T0195076

A
SIMPLE
MATTER
OF
HOPE
AND
JOY

NATHAN MENOIAN

authorHOUSE®

AuthorHouse™
1663 Liberty Drive
Bloomington, IN 47403
www.authorhouse.com
Phone: 833-262-8899

Published by AuthorHouse 07/29/2021

ISBN: 978-1-6655-1564-1 (sc)
ISBN: 978-1-6655-1567-2 (e)

Library of Congress Control Number: 2021901860

Print information available on the last page.

Any people depicted in stock imagery provided by Getty Images are models,
and such images are being used for illustrative purposes only.
Certain stock imagery © Getty Images.

This book is printed on acid-free paper.

Because of the dynamic nature of the Internet, any web addresses or
links contained in this book may have changed since publication and
may no longer be valid. The views expressed in this work are solely those
of the author and do not necessarily reflect the views of the publisher,
and the publisher hereby disclaims any responsibility for them.

Plus, the Bible scriptures used in the manuscript are The
Holy Bible, New International Version, NIV Copyright
1973,1978,1984,2011,by Biblica, Inc. TM

Scripture taken from the Holy Bible, New International Version®. Copyright ©
1973, 1978, 1984 Biblica. Used by permission of Zondervan. All rights reserved.

1

December turns Michigan prettier than one can imagine. With shimmering snowflakes, Christmas trees, smiling faces, holiday lights, and happy carolers, the traditional wintry images and season's greetings are a delight. Overall, a great backdrop to dig in and start writing about my newly changed life.

I had the plot, purpose, and people all planned out. The many hours I spent writing each day passed without notice. My words were plentiful, and the keyboard on my laptop took quite a beating.

As soft as my writing skills were, I worked feverishly hard at improving them, and for good reason; I was a new man with a changed heart. Behind these recent occurrences is a worthwhile story. It contains a moral perspective, a heart of truth, a bit of mystery, and a happy ending.

At the outset, I took inventory of my state-of-mind. As much as the next guy, I was alright. But I was now middle-aged and no longer up to fighting my way through life. Was it time to move over, giving way to the next generation?

Finish up, clean up, lie down and die: Quite a grim outcome and one I didn't want to fulfill.

There must be more to life than working and paying bills: more than a good night's sleep and more than good food. What I sought after was a real and tangible substance; definitely nothing man-made or rooted in soil. If I did find such a beautiful gift, I'd somehow want to share it with the world.

Hope! It has always existed, but not easy to find. It's a powerful, impactful, and everlasting word that needs to be shared. If possible, my heart's desire would be to write about it, talk about it, and live in it.

The lady who owns my heart agreed with my noble intentions: "Offering hope through Jesus Christ is worth every effort," she said. "What better way is there to live our lives? Tell it straight, and tell it true."

"I'll do my best," I readily assured her.

Whenever life agitates my emotions, I close my eyes and sink into the calming power of God's handiwork, a precious comfort afforded me as a new believer in Jesus Christ. Country meadows become the perfect retreat.

Such exquisite landscapes are a tiny sliver of heaven on Earth. I walk through them as slow as a vacationing tourist. The invisible wind makes my impromptu visits there more pleasant. Fragrant hints of lavender, lilac, mint, pine, lemon balm, and distant rosebuds sneak through the air.

For a few moments, and sometimes longer, I pause to watch winsome leaves on sturdy trees shake and giggle like laughing children. In just minutes my emotions are calm again.

My race through life is now more than half over, and

to my astonishment, I am still up and running. Are there others, I've wondered, who might be surprised at their own longevity?

After twenty years of running a business and chasing success, I somehow lost my zest for life. Pride kept me chained to my work, and it cost me a pretty penny. Little in life seemed worth fighting for. I later discovered I was wrong about that.

Running a business is wickedly time-consuming, and mine was no different. One thing I made every effort to do was keep my social calendar open for occasional dating, and monthly get-togethers with some of my long-time buddies.

I'm of the opinion that 21st-century living has become a ruthless fight for survival. Looking back over my battles and having the scars to prove it, I've survived tough times, fought and outlasted nasty enemies, stayed ahead of the rat race, and laughed at close calls.

I'm honestly not that tough of a person, but I do believe someone has been watching over me: Perhaps one or two large-winged guardian angels.

If a video from the past few years of my life existed, it would reveal an uneventful and routine span of time. My head-first slide into middle-age was awkward and funny looking. My wardrobe never varied from dark pants, white shirts, black socks, and plain leather shoes. I pretty much ate the same meals at the same restaurants, and rarely changed my TV viewing habits. For me, that lifestyle worked.

Saturday mornings found me tending to the household chores: vacuuming, dusting, washing dishes, and doing laundry. When all of that was done, I'd drive into town to fill my car up with gas, and then meet friends for breakfast.

Beyond the rigors of daily life, slept the neglected details of my spiritual condition, mostly void of anything to do with the Creator. Though I usually described myself as a nonbeliever, it would have been more accurate to say that I just didn't get along with God. I foolishly pushed Him aside wanting to prove that I could take care of myself.

Not surprisingly, and because of my stubborn spirit, there were a good number of lessons in life I had to learn the hard way. All I cared about was what I wanted. That was my attitude, and never did I feel it was wrong. Then I had the audacity to ask God for a miracle. What kind of fool would do that? Do prayers from the likes of me ever garner God's attention?

I'm not a gambling man, but I know that you can't win if you don't play. My selfish prayer was more along the lines of covering the odds. If I overlooked repeating it at least once a month, I'd feel guilty.

"Lord, please grab hold of me and lift me out of the deep ruts I keep getting stuck in. And if you will, kindly position me in close proximity to a woman that may need my help in some form or fashion. Thank you. Amen."

Did I really expect a miracle? My answer was always the same: "You just never know." I must have repeated that dozens of times to as many people. I was starting to believe it myself.

Then one morning, and right in front of me, something unspectacular took place. Yes, unspectacular. But because of it, I was miraculously and forever changed.

During a recent gas-station visit, a mid-sized sedan wobbled in on a flat tire. I watched as the female driver headed over to the air pump, shut off the engine, and step out of the car. She was smartly-dressed and very attractive. I wondered what she was going to do about her dilemma.

I, however, knew what I was going to do. This stunningly pretty woman, whose name I didn't yet know, moved me beyond my senses. My chivalrous instincts immediately kicked in as I bee-lined straight over to her, offering my assistance. She gladly accepted.

Right then and there, my 'hoped-for' miracle materialized in the blink of an eye. No way was I going to let this opportunity pass without a valiant effort to, at least, pursue conversation with her. While changing the flat tire, my anxious thoughts focused on inviting her out. I also took a quick glance at her hands looking for a ring. Not even one!

Something was coming alive in me. I found a cause worth fighting for. With my work done and a few scraped knuckles and light smears of tire grit and grime on my hands, I bravely asked if she might care to join me for breakfast.

"I'd love to!" She said. "But it'll be my treat."

The lady standing in front of me didn't know this yet, but I was too old-fashioned to let that happen. Nothing about this occurrence was premeditated on my part. I was in the right place at the right time. But was there another explanation, besides mere coincidence, for my sudden good fortune?

Accepting my suggestion on where to eat, she followed me to the Pancake Palace, kitty-corner from the gas station. We trailed a perky hostess to a corner booth and placed our order. It wasn't long before our pancakes arrived. We buttered them fast and drenched them with hot syrup. Just as I was about to dig in, my guest bowed her head in prayer.

"Jesus, I thank you for our food this morning, and please bless this very nice man who changed my tire. Amen."

It had been years since I prayed before a meal. Though I was impressed with her religious courage, I wasn't sure why she felt the need to pray in a public setting. But who was I to question a person about matters of faith, especially someone I barely knew.

I picked up my fork, ready to eat again, when she asked my name. A fair request, which made me wonder why I hadn't already told her. But before I could answer, she exclaimed that pancakes were among her favorite morning foods.

Hoping to impress her, I ad-libbed a mushy response. "Anyone who loves pancakes can't be too bad. You must have a very kind heart."

She sent a flattering comment right back. "Well then, I guess you can't be too bad either with that mountain of hotcakes in front of you. And, by the way, I'm Marsha Kelly."

My hand met hers half-way across the table for a gentle handshake, and that's when I shared my name. "Eric David Matthews," I said, wanting the whole of it to sound more impressive.

Her attractiveness was a bit of distraction. More than a couple of times, instead of paying attention to what she was saying, I caught myself gazing with childlike-wonder into her blue and shiny eyes. Thankfully she didn't seem bothered by my superficial conduct.

We finished up eating and took to drinking our coffee. "Are you from around here?" She asked, leaning slowly back in the booth.

"I live in Milford, one straight mile down the road from where we sit right now." I paused and asked where she lived.

"Detroit! The Motor City. And thank you again, Mr. Eric David Matthews, for changing my tire. You truly blessed me." Her kind words sounded believable. In repeating back my full name I knew she had me pegged.

As we continued chatting, Marsha became more relaxed. I wanted to do the same, but my insides were much too jumpy and nervous.

"What brings you out this way?" My innocent question brought a smile to her face.

"Truth be told, I'm on a mission looking for souls to save."

"Well, don't look at me," I said stoically. "I'm beyond saving. The sins I'm guilty of have surely sealed my fate. My life isn't anything God would be interested in."

Displaying no reaction to my professed lack of faith, Marsha began sharing her story. Without a hint of arrogance in her voice, she spoke convincingly of her Christian faith. I liked what I heard.

Glancing at the large clock on the wall behind the cash register, I realized we'd been there nearly two hours. And surprisingly, Marsha seemed in no hurry to leave. But no matter, I wanted nothing more than to remain gazing into her wonderful blue eyes.

Before leaving, we exchanged phone numbers. She handed me hers on a slip of paper, which sweetly included her full name: Marsha Sarah Kelly.

2

Refreshing waves of happy emotions washed over me as I headed home from the restaurant. I probably shook my head three or four times in disbelief, wondering if the past few hours had been a dream.

The living room was where I did my best thinking, with all of its comfortable furniture. But for this situation, instead of heading to the couch, I paced the floor with purposed steps. I was no stranger to love-at-first-sight, if that's what this was. Yet, never once did any of those escapades develop into a lasting relationship.

I had no idea what to expect regarding Marsha. In contemplating her devout faith, I knew my usual dating strategy would need adjusting, and the reasons were clear. Marsha was not one to be taken lightly, and was different in ways I didn't fully understand. Her life-changing words stirred my soul. I truly wanted to become friends with this marvelous Christian lady.

Marsha was unlike any woman I had ever known or dated. But how do I date a saint? How and where do I learn the proper etiquette for such an endeavor? A seed of new wonderment was galloping around in my heart. Moments like that don't just happen. What was going on? Was this another miracle from God?

Earlier in the week, I had made plans for this particular evening to get together with friends. A conflicting thought interrupted me. Might God be upset if I didn't stay home to spend 'getting acquainted' time with Him, especially in light of what He had done for me earlier in the day?

I wasn't saying no to Him, but wasn't close to saying yes. I didn't know how to put my potential faith into action. Was I supposed to get down on my knees and pray? Or could I still go out with my friends and respectfully catch up with God later?

Considering all of my imperfections, I didn't see much sense in actively pursuing God. With all of His perfection, why would He want anything to do with me? A questioning mindset had always been my excuse for keeping God at arm's length. Bottled-up inside of me were questions I wanted to ask Him: Who, what, where, when, how, and why were just the tip of the iceberg. Until He answered those concerns, disrespectful as they probably were, I certainly wasn't going to run after Him.

Though I could never explain to anyone what happened next, God silenced my questions, replacing them with peace and trust. In my opinion, that was a miracle. Immediately saying goodnight to my evening plans, I freely surrendered all of my attention to Him.

Totally unable to figure out how He secretly orchestrated the dozens of details in bringing Marsha and me to the same place, on the same day, at the same time; I still ended up changing her flat tire, and she ended up telling me about her faith in Jesus Christ.

A glimpse of the big picture began taking shape in my spirit. That's when my overall attitude about God began to soften. I felt my knees weaken. Before falling flat on my face, I hurried over to the couch and stretched-out flat.

A blast of hard-hitting thoughts attacked me. The first was a blunt reminder of the harsh coldness I displayed toward anyone I didn't care about and hoped to avoid. Other shaming faults, just as unpleasant, came to light.

I was experiencing new thoughts about the invisible God, and confronted with serious questions. My eternal destination was being decided. "What was my responsibility in all of this, and who was I to expect a guiding hand from God?" These were honest questions that carried their own truth.

It was to my life-long detriment that I would over-analyze, second-guess, and cease believing anything I couldn't personally attest to. In the same way, that was my attitude about God. How stupid of me.

I sensed something divine was about to happen. It did! Faster than I could have imagined, God opened the eyes of my grumpy heart to His compassion and love. He showed me humanity in motion, each person precious and priceless in His sight, blessed with a free-will and warmly-welcomed into having spiritual intimacy with The Creator.

A blaring trumpet rallied my weary soul to attention! A surge of hope and joy flooded into my heart. Most wondrously, I realized that I was not beyond His reach! With absolute certainty, I now believed in a caring and miracle-working God!

These quick and sweet occurrences were nothing short

of spectacular. The face on this miracle belonged to Marsha Kelly, whose personal story of faith led me to believe that she was well-aligned with her God, knew of what she spoke, and lived it.

Life as I knew it would rapidly be changing. How could it not? God was pointing me towards the path of a searching saint and away from the godless thoughts, habits, and desires of the wayward sinner I had long been. None of this was easy to grasp.

I knew at some point, the cynical side of me would rear its ugly head. God wouldn't use a flat tire and pancakes to strong-arm someone into believing in Him, would He? Was Marsha part of the plan?

True, I nearly did lose control of my thoughts while in her presence. I thought it was just infatuation; maybe I was wrong. Marsha's joy and trust in God made me keenly aware of my disappointments, sadness, and flaming eruptions of distress that I have never spoken about to anyone.

Even with limited success in life, I dreamed of having more. But failure after failure buried me within cement walls of life's hard realities. I was a grown man sinking in his own foolishness.

Was Marsha tossing me an invisible lifeline to grab hold of? Might I be in some approaching spiritual danger? Was I headed for a fall just before crossing the finish line in a race to redemption? Were hellfire and brimstone just ahead of me?

Until this point, my thoughts had been worldly. If Marsha wasn't as pretty as she was, it would have been 'see you later' with no invitation to breakfast, and probably not even an offer to change her tire. How shallow of me.

As I was about to get up from the couch, a few ridiculous thoughts snuck into my brain. I laughingly and quickly dismissed them. Marsha is not an alien from outer space. And no, I am not under any spell of hers.

Those sneaky and foolish thoughts grew calm, as the Lord put before me another 'tiny sliver' of heaven, where His peace is so overwhelming. The quiet green hills and flowering landscapes relax and soothe my soul.

Springtime brings us chirping birds and blossoming trees. A bit poetic sounding, perhaps, but isn't that what love can be all about?

Why am I bringing love into this? Was it because I had fallen head-over-heels for a stranger? I don't believe so. Way-back-when, I hoped for one little miracle with my name on it to change me for the better, nothing more. The Creator of the Universe wanted to give me something beyond that. That's His way of being God.

Was I anywhere near ready for more life-changing miracles? From my landline phone, I punched in Marsha's number. There was much for us to talk about.

To my dismay, the call went unanswered. I didn't bother leaving a message. At that moment, I hated the thought of wanting to fall in love with Marsha or anyone.

3

Sometime during the next week, I felt brave enough to call Marsha again. Her magic was unpredictable, and I couldn't tell what might happen if she answered this time. Just in case, I jotted down some notes. Good thing, too.

The moment I heard her sweet voice, I nearly did forget the reason for my call. I took a hurried glance at my note pad. The words rushed out of me, "Would you like to join me for dinner?"

I was nearly speechless when she accepted my invitation. Our get-together would be at a popular steak house evenly distanced between Detroit and Milford. Five o'clock was the agreed-upon time.

The words, 'Not a doubting Thomas', came back to mind. I gave her the happy highlights.

"All that you shared at breakfast last Saturday deeply touched me. That night, the Lord grabbed hold of my heart. He graciously allowed me to ask Him all sorts of questions, and patiently waited as I pitifully attempted to explain away all the excuses I had for ignoring Him.

"God told me how much He loved me. I was overwhelmed

by this encounter, and experienced a powerful rush of hope and joy racing through my veins.

"Life has suddenly felt exciting again. And Marsha, all of this happened because you told me what Jesus has done in your life."

She spoke softly. "Wow, I'm crying. I didn't expect to hear all this so soon after just meeting you."

A wind of change was coming over me. I personally wanted to acknowledge Jesus in my life, but not give up chasing Marsha. My conscience, though, made it clear that He was to be the top priority.

On the day of our date, I arrived a few minutes early, waiting anxiously in the lobby for Marsha, who arrived on time. After a quick embrace, we were shown to a table.

Living single for many years caused me to be less concerned about prim and proper behavior. Though when dining in the company of such a classy lady as Marsha, I knew it would be most important to eat slowly, take small bites, and make good use of my table napkin.

"Try to act sophisticated," I reminded myself. "Don't show yourself as a flophouse bachelor. Above all else, refrain from trying to sound clever and witty; definitely one of my faults."

After a dinner prayer from Marsha, her next words jolted me. "God put you on my mind this week." Her voice was very matter-of-fact.

"What on Earth for?" I asked, more than surprised.

Being the reserved woman she seemed to be, I figured Marsha wouldn't admit if her heart did a little jump and jig when we first met. But that particular morning, she was on a divine mission, and there wasn't room for anything other than, 'mission accomplished.'

Marsha finished another bite of steak before handing me an intriguing revelation. "When you told me how God grabbed hold of your heart, I sensed in my spirit that doors of evangelism will open for you.

"God will give you the words to speak. I don't know how soon, but in the months ahead I believe you're going to be a busy man. It'll be important for you to pray about this without ceasing."

I sat quiet for a minute. Her words were humbling, bringing me to confess that I needed to learn more about prayer.

"Prayer is acknowledging God's authority, greatness, and of course His Deity," she explained. "We ask for guidance, wisdom, and material things, etc. Whether you're talking one-on-one with Him or sounding churchy and formal, it's all prayer. Always be honest and respectful to Him.

"And remember, listening is of equal importance while in prayer. God may speak words to you. Bottom line, prayer helps deepen our faith. Stay diligent in reading the Bible, as it will instruct and lead you in His ways. The Bible holds the answers to life's problems."

Marsha ended her answer with a tender smile. We continued eating in comfortable silence. Should the opportunity arise, how might I ever describe this marvelous woman to my friends? I am a richer man for knowing her.

After the table plates were cleared away, Marsha squared back her shoulders and cleared her throat. "Now please don't laugh at this," she said, "but I secretly wished that we could have danced together the morning we first met. Even a ten-second waltz would have filled me with overwhelming joy."

Her words literally pushed me back in my chair. If I had said anything questioning her soundness, she would have been heartbroken.

I couldn't hide my enthusiasm. "Marsha, I'm no prime-time dancer, but a Pancake Palace waltz was definitely doable! You're a special lady with great faith. Attractive as you are, I imagine you're probably asked out quite often."

A shy and embarrassed look hijacked her gorgeous face. She shook her head, "Eric, you'd be surprised at how rarely I date."

Hearing that, I realized I was one of the fortunate few. It was the moment I was hoping for. She apparently found me likable.

Even as a devout Christian, she wasn't afraid to show herself as vulnerable. That brand of honesty connected with me. I firmly believed that Marsha was steady and strong in her faith, and would never abandon it.

A probing question jumped into my brain, and for a moment I held back asking it. She might take it the wrong way. I proceeded with caution. "Is it possible to be sold out to God, as you are, and still enjoy a social life?"

Marsha took a slow sip of coffee, as her eyes locked onto mine. What she shared touched my heart. "I've always wanted to be a wife and a mother," she confided. "But my life has turned out much differently. There were times I've felt lonely watching so many of my friends find love and get married. I've asked God when it would be my turn."

It was twenty years earlier when she began seeking concrete answers about life. Marsha was not raised in church, nor had any amount of religious instruction. She lived unaware of God's greatness.

Marsha filled in the details of how she came to know Jesus Christ. "I earned my teaching certificate and degree for Middle School English Literature, composition, and grammar.

"Things were looking good for me as I started my career, but within a month I was blindsided by two things that broke my heart into a hundred pieces. I lost my closest friend to cancer. Then, shortly afterward, I had to put Sugar, my French Poodle, down.

"I wanted truthful answers that would bring comfort to my heart. My first attempt was to find out if there was a merciful God who knew my name, and did He love me?

"I wound up reading the first four books of The New Testament: Matthew, Mark, Luke, and John. I was not disappointed," she said. "Since then, I haven't stopped reading the Bible.

"Amazingly, I found out much about Jesus: Where did He come from? What did He do on Earth? Why did He go to the Cross? What did He accomplish on the Cross? Is He alive? Where is He now? Is He coming back?

"My faith was growing, and I gladly invited Him into my heart," Marsha shared as her eyes moistened. "I had become a born-again Christian and a new creature in Christ. I found what I was looking for."

For a blur of a moment, I peered into my own future. I stood at a crossroad seeing God straight ahead of Marsha, and me cowering off to the side. I also wasn't surprised to see the familiar and ugly face of doubt hiding in the shadows. What was I to make of that scenario?

There was so much more I wanted to talk to her about. I asked if she might agree to another date.

"How about going to a coffee shop?" She suggested. "There's an all-nighter around the corner."

"Great!" I said, taking care of the dinner tab and tip. "And let's have some dessert there too."

The coffee shop was nearly empty when we walked in. A smiling waitress was quick to take our order.

"I'm glad we have more time to talk," Marsha remarked, as coffee and cake were set in front of us.

"These past few days have been a whirlwind for me. This evening is an answer to prayer, and gives me a short break from the things I've been praying about. I'm in over my head on most of them.

"One in particular is about moving out of state. I love teaching fifth and sixth graders. Ohio and Virginia have posted several positions for experienced elementary teachers, and I applied for both. This all sounds promising, yet there are a lot of details to be considered."

I was impressed by her openness and how freely both of us shared the personal side of our thoughts, hers more than mine.

Having a miserable lack of biblical knowledge, I wondered if there was another way to impress Marsha, but nothing spiritual came to mind. My only chance then was to use personal charm, a risky effort for sure.

Unknowingly, Marsha let me off the hook. Her timing was excellent. In the blink of an eye, she changed the direction of our conversation with a simple request: "May I put you on the spot with personal questions?"

"Ask away!" I said.

"What do you think of marriage?" A caution flag went up in my mind.

"Marriage is good."

"Have you been married?"

"Yes, but am divorced."

"Children?"

"Two wonderful sons."

"If you were to marry again, would you want more?"

"At my age, grandchildren are what I want."

"How old are you?" She asked without hesitation.

"54."

"Would you consider relocating?"

"That's a tough one. I love Michigan."

"Are you in good financial shape for a second marriage?"

"Money is not a problem."

Before letting Marsha ask anything else, I politely interrupted her: "May I have a turn?"

"Okay, you're up!" She said, smiling and rubbing her hands together.

My questions would be fast and furious, but all in fun. Hopefully, I might discover things we have in common.

Marsha leaned in across the table. I did the same. Would she be up to answering questions that had nothing to do with her faith? I hoped so.

"Who do you like more, The Beatles or Rolling Stones?"

"The Beatles."

"Baseball or hockey?"

"Baseball."

"Football or basketball?"

"Neither."

"Fried eggs or scrambled?"

"Either. But both are always better with pancakes."
Marsha was keeping up just fine.

"Which one, Winter or Summer?"

"For sure, Summer."

"Chess, Checkers, or Backgammon?"

"Backgammon."

"Cats or dogs?"

"Cats."

"Pepsi or Coke?"

"Root Beer."

"C'mon. Gotta choose."

"Coke."

"Me too," I said, in full agreement.

"Bowling or billiards?"

"Bowling."

"Walking or running?"

"Walking."

"Here's my last question for now. I promise."

"Norman Rockwell or Michelangelo?"

"Both."

"Pick one."

"Okay then, Picasso!"

We both let out a laugh. At that very moment I became all hers. Where else would I ever find such a lady with such a heart?

"Hey, that was fun," she remarked. "Okay, it's my turn again. Be honest now."

"Monopoly or Clue?"

"Monopoly."

"Artificial Christmas tree or real?"

"REAL."

"CD's or vinyl?"

"Vinyl."

"Comedy or drama?"

"Comedy."

"It's a Wonderful Life or A Christmas Story?"

"It's a Wonderful Life."

In an instant, the tone in her voice turned serious, so did the look on her face.

"Protestant or Catholic?" She asked.

"Protestant."

"Now here's a tough one."

"King James Bible or the New International Version?"

"Not fair."

"Why?"

"I haven't read either of them," I admitted with shame.

Marsha was a tough interrogator. Her questions made me think.

"Does God have a sense of humor?" She queried.

I was sure of my answer. "Yes!"

"God loves you because you are good, or because He is good?"

"He is good."

"Jesus forgives us because we deserve His mercy or because He is merciful?"

"He is merciful."

"Does God need us, or do we need Him?"

"We need Him."

"Is God's love conditional or unconditional?"

"Unconditional."

Though I was mostly guessing, apparently my biblical answers were right. Marsha didn't correct a single one. The next moment between us was quiet. I couldn't think of anything to say.

We simultaneously looked at each other, realizing something special had just happened. I hoped the good feeling in my heart would last beyond the night.

Marsha spoke up. "Neither of us could have planned how nice this evening has turned out. This is proof God is good. I want to pray with you before we go home tonight, Eric. Would that be alright?"

"Absolutely!" I answered. "And will you lead me in the sinner's prayer? I want to start out on the right foot, so to speak."

This woman was a godsend. I truly wanted to know more about her, especially who she was when not looking for souls to save. Marsha must have been reading my mind.

"I'm a person with many sides to my personality," she said, still leaning in towards me. "One thing you may have noticed is that I enjoy people with a good sense of humor. I like to think that I can be humorous too.

"I tell you honestly, being able to laugh is drastically important in life today. Such serious issues confront us on many topics. Without laughter and time to enjoy the lighter moments in life, well, we'd all be zombies."

Sitting across from me was the lady of my dreams. I wondered what I'd ever done to deserve being in her company. Without being told, I knew it was all God's doing.

I wanted a serious relationship with Marsha; I just had no idea how to reach her heart. Such an amazing and wonderful woman: One, perhaps, I could marry?

Regardless of romantic pursuits, I would need to put God first. I was anxious for Marsha to pray the night to a close, leading me in the prayer that would make me a new man.

She asked me to repeat her words. "Jesus, I need to be saved. I invite you into my heart to rule and reign over my life. Please forgive me of all my sins, and wash me in the precious blood you shed for me. I receive your free gift of salvation and willingly surrender and submit to you. Use me for your glory. Thank you, Jesus! Amen."

No other moment in my life, up to that point and time, could compare. I was a new man!

4

Nobody is perfect, I reminded myself, but Marsha Sarah Kelly was pushing the envelope. She was likely the most complete woman I'd ever met. It was truly refreshing to know a lady who didn't think more highly of herself than she ought to; another of her rare traits.

If ever there was such a thing as a personality resume; hers would include wisdom, kindness, joy, love, humor, and integrity.

Our first date went so remarkably well that I couldn't keep myself from replaying it. My heart and brain traded off highlights of the evening.

I loved how Marsha never once, that entire evening, made me uncomfortable about being biblically illiterate.

She was impressively kind, humble, and eloquent. Marsha was a quiet reflection of charm and poise.

She effortlessly held her head high and never looked awkward doing so. Her shoulders were always straight, nearly military. And at my next observation, I chuckled, but it impressed me, she sipped from her water glass very ladylike. Her every move resonated graceful motion. And at no point was her voice any louder than it ought to have been.

I was honored that she trusted me enough to share her vulnerabilities. It was flattering to know she wished for a breakfast dance the morning we first met.

There were more personal confessions. Marsha had always been single and came to accept it, but couldn't stop hating the heavy 'chain of loneliness' tormenting her heart.

I was lonely too. No way out and no way up. A slight exaggeration perhaps, but when Marsha talked about the 'chain of loneliness,' my ears opened up. Our thoughts and emotions were similar.

My life without Christ had been a mess. With Christ, Marsha's life was spent going God's way. The most impactful thing was her intense love for God. Her voice softened whenever she spoke out from her heart; "I live for God," she said. "I love reading and studying the Bible. I believe it, and obey it."

Marsha expressed great joy over how much God loves her. Then, without much of a pause, added how totally undeserving she was of that love. Her mature faith made me aware that I had a long way to go before becoming her spiritual equal. Sit, listen, and learn was pretty much all I could do.

As she continued, Marsha sweetly revealed that she had been baptized in the Holy Spirit - with the evidence of speaking in other tongues. I was unfamiliar with that aspect of God, but was hungry for all of His promises.

Marsha's eyes suddenly filled with tears. Something she hadn't planned on sharing tumbled out.

"Maybe they were just innocently teasing," I said, upon

hearing of it. Marsha wasn't as sure and lowered her voice to barely a whisper.

"A few months ago, some of the newer teachers at school asked me if I was play-acting in being faithful-to-a-fault and was I as true-of-a-friend as others there had said about me?

"Perhaps that was their way of chiding me for being so 'saintly'; something that seemed to bring on a few condescending laughs. They hadn't known me long at all. I was hurt by their questions."

I couldn't imagine Marsha being anything other than a faithful friend. She would be the one that stood with you when others turned and ran. And, if for no other reason, she wanted to remain as steadfast as Jesus.

"How difficult is it for you as a teacher, to be a student at the feet of Jesus?" I asked, wanting her confident voice to return.

"It's quite easy!" She exclaimed. "That's where I have learned deep and wonderful things. My service to Him is all about being a student. Maintaining a disciplined prayer life, which includes times of fasting, keeps me in close communication with Jesus.

"I know for a fact that learning never ceases, especially when the expert you're learning from is the Creator of the Universe! Our conversations are always life lessons. It is the best education I ever imagined getting." Her confident voice was back again.

Marsha's exuberant words touched me. I felt a few tears trying to escape my eyes, but I wouldn't dare release them in front of her. Crying in front of a woman just seemed out of the question for me. I imagine though, if one small drop had fallen out, her quick compassion would have stood to the ready.

Between too many cups of coffee that night, we chatted, laughed, and shared from our hearts. If possible, I'd somehow love to gain possession of the booth we occupied there as a happy memento.

It was in the parking lot where she and I hugged goodnight. She asked me to wait a moment before leaving, then reached into her car and brought out a red folder.

"Take a read through this," she said, handing it to me. "It needs polishing up, but let me know if it resonates with you. I'm hoping to include some of this in a book I'm writing."

I made my way home in light traffic. The red folder occupied the passenger seat, sending a hint of Marsha's fruity perfume through the car. This was one evening I would not forget, nor want to: A perfect date with a perfect lady.

5

Trucks and Tools, as I originally named my business, had grown to eight large facilities throughout Lower Michigan. We were a rental operation for the obvious things; trucks and tools, plus a growing variety of handy gadgets for home and shop.

Customers were continually telling me it was a dynamite place to do business. After five years of explosive growth, I boldly renamed it T&T. I was told to include a disclaimer, 'no dynamite available': A legal thing.

In my heart, letting go of this 'baby' wasn't even a possibility. I worked hard to build the company with two decades of sweat, toil, and blood, nearly draining my soul. What might happen to me if I sold the business? I'd lose my identity. That was enough to keep me from considering any offer, even though I was tempted.

Things change. My focus slowly shifted from being completely immersed in the business, to wanting a newer purpose in life with less stress and more peace. Were such lofty expectations realistic? I was hopeful. At my age, any opportunity to lift myself to higher levels was intriguing.

During this same time, I received a registered letter from a college buddy of mine, Donovan Steele, living in Virginia. He was coming to Michigan soon, hoping we could meet for dinner. There would be a lot of catching up to do.

I was now stepping full-time into life as a new and nervous believer, ready to follow Jesus wherever He might lead.

Afraid of bothering Him with a silly question, I asked it of myself. "How does a person muster up enough courage to wear a shiny badge identifying them as a 'born-again' Christian?" I needed to feel comfortable in my new skin.

What I did next totally surprised me. Standing in the middle of my living room, I began shouting: "I'm a born-again Christian! I'm a born-again Christian!"

Had I gone off my rocker? Was this behavior really necessary? I kept that up for five-minutes, leaving my throat raw and my face covered with sweat. The image of myself doing this made me laugh.

When I stopped, I whispered a raspy-sounding prayer: "Lord, forgive me for acting foolish. What do I do with this new and wonderful life you've given me?"

My heart truly desires to serve Him on a daily basis, all or nothing. Doing so was another story.

I carried no premeditated sermon in my pocket. If I were to cross paths with family or friends, they surely wouldn't care to hear about my new life, I timidly reasoned, especially knowing of their general disbelief in God.

How might I share God's plan of salvation with people who use vulgar language and mock those who believe in Jesus? Amazing to me was the fact that not long ago, I too was a doubter with no regard for the eternal destination of my soul.

"Are you sure you want me telling others of your greatness?" I questioned the Lord. When imperfection speaks of perfection, what might result? I could only wonder.

Marsha's prophetic words came back to me: "Jesus will open doors for you to share your faith." What doors was she talking about?

Overly anxious to start running on the new legs of faith beneath me, my teetering motions resembled a newborn foal wobbling side-to-side, but rarely forward. For a short period, baby-steps would be my daily regimen.

Interestingly, things I once thought of as miracles were now part of my daily Christian life, just one month new. I smile in awe as God makes life's simple things into memorable moments. Was meeting Marsha my first miracle, or was it her pointing me towards Jesus Christ? My heart would finish the story.

I wondered if I possessed any noticeable outward sign identifying me as a changed man. My bathroom mirror revealed nothing of the sort.

The brown eyes in my head were no different, and nothing about my voice had changed. I had no priestly garb, no change in hair color, or change in my wide grin.

I did, though, feel an inward change one day when a sprig of patience broke through my encrusted heart while inching along in a slow-moving line at the bank. A week earlier and I'd have been fuming with impatience.

From day-too-day, my head swelled with questions about Christian living. Even going to church gave me pause. I understood very little about God, and in a spiritual sense that was frightening. Finding a church to join was going to be difficult, but necessary. I soon found one that took me in.

I've listened to more than one money-hungry TV preacher instructing me on how to 'name it and claim it.' I actually tried that once, but that dark-blue Lincoln Continental never showed up in my driveway. How stupid could I be? I laughed at myself. If God gave us everything we wanted, can you imagine the mess the world would be in?

Marsha was the only person I knew that had come through the gauntlet of screaming preachers and spiritual hucksters. The religious marketplace was not where I wanted to learn about God.

Whatever my life was supposed to be as a Christian, I hadn't yet come close to understanding how to mesh everyday life and faith into a seamless existence.

I was putting my new life together with random pieces all out of order, unable to decipher the instruction booklet. Was faith alone in Jesus Christ a ticket to a problem-free life? Would scripture expose me as a fool?

Reading the Bible intimidated me. Was scripture heaven-sent or human-made? Could I understand the Bible? I suppose my excuses delighted the devil.

The old me fought the new me. Living for God would not be a cakewalk. I had to settle the matter and take the plunge.

Yes! It would be God all the way. Going through life hand-in-hand with the Creator of the Universe would be a marvelous journey! He isn't looking at the dust and dirt on my face, but rather the light shining through me from His touch.

"Human perfection isn't possible," Marsha said during our first meal together. "But never stop working towards being the best you can be in Him."

A short prayer formed in my heart. I had to speak it. "Lord, please don't let me mess up and disappoint you. Help me to pay attention to your guidance. Open up my brain and pour into it the things you want me to know about you. Amen."

That same night, as I lay down for sleep, a strange vision scrolled before me. Was I dreaming?

A street preacher was calling out to passersby to consider their eternal destination. I couldn't make out his face. When he was done sermonizing, he knelt to pray alongside a hurting soul wearing a messy flood of tears, and confessing aloud his many sins.

That's who the preacher was there for. Was I that preacher? I woke from the dream, nervous and troubled. For a moment it seemed okay to distance myself from the vision. It was unimaginable to me that God saw anything worthwhile or usable in my human condition; flawed, cracked, and tarnished as it was.

If there was a possibility of God calling me into service, my defiant attitude wasn't anything He couldn't overcome. During the next few months the dream replayed itself, gently stirring my heart.

6

The next get-together with my friends was right around the corner. I had excused myself from the previous rendezvous; as that was the night I spent getting better acquainted with God. That also was the day I first met Marsha.

I looked forward to these monthly events, as we each had become true-blue friends over the years. The host-homes were chosen on a rotating basis, and the evening's activities were kept secret until all had arrived.

The grilling of steaks, chops, burgers, sausages, and an occasional mystery-meat were the most popular of our gatherings: A backyard blast for all concerned.

Aside from cookouts, we would play a night of poor-man's poker. No bet over one dollar. Other times, we might watch a championship game on TV, attend a movie, or have a guitar-jam and sing along.

This particular night at Sid Jackson's house would be fun. He had things set up for a poker game, with plenty of snacks and beverages close at hand.

Sid was also the guitar player among us. On more than

one occasion, when we ran out of energy during the evening, he re-energized us with a few up-tempo songs.

Though I was quietly apprehensive about it, I did join in the games that night. My prayer for the evening was a short one; "Lord Jesus, please help me know the right time to bring You into the conversation."

Near the end of the evening, and to my astonishment, Sid put forth an unusual proposition: "Gentlemen, instead of going home now, why don't we spend a few minutes talking about something other than women, work, drinking, and sports?"

Whatever had caused him to want a new level of conversation was alright with me. As it turned out, the guys had nothing new to talk about. I would soon be changing that.

Jim Stevens spoke up first. He managed an auto body paint shop and was the group's resident complainer. "What else can I say? It's the same mess all the time for me. The owner is a royal jerk, and I work with a gang of incompetent people all day long. Beyond that, life is just a bowl of cherries."

"Well, I've got something here that's more positive," Gary Owens said. "My week went pretty well. All of my students turned their assignments in on time. American History, you may well know, isn't the easiest subject to teach ninth graders. But it does appear as though they're getting the material down pretty well."

The time had arrived. I was ready, but nervous. Right before me stood one of those 'doors' pushed open by the Hand of God. I jumped in with both feet, not sure what anyone's reaction would be.

"Okay gentlemen, listen up. When you die, where will you spend eternity, in heaven or hell?"

My pointed question caught everyone off guard. A silent pause accompanied their gaggle of weird stares. We usually agreed on most issues, but this new topic revealed some hidden differences.

"You want to know what?" Sid asked in a sarcastic voice. "Who goes where when they die?"

I kept at it. "I'm serious! Each of us is going to die. We all know that, right? Have any of you given thought as to where you will spend eternity?"

Sid answered back. "I'll tell you where I'm going when I die, right straight to hell. I just can't picture myself anywhere else; playing the harp and floating on a cloud doesn't fit me. I'd be more a keeper of Hell's flames.

"The devil isn't such a bad guy. I think he gets a bad rap. And how bad will hell be since that's where most people will probably end up?" His comments were not original. History has heard them before.

Bob Greene, a CPA, confessed that he didn't know how to get to heaven, but hell was not for him. "I do not want to end up there. That place is nothing but darkness, torment, heat, and sadness. There's no way I want to be around that. I do not want to spend eternity in hell."

It was fascinating to hear these men talk honestly about such a serious topic. And I wasn't too surprised by what I was hearing. Only once, years before, had we shared our religious beliefs in front of the others. At that point, there wasn't an ounce of Christian faith between any of us. In no way though, did that mean we weren't kind-hearted or void of compassion.

This night was different; I was now a follower of Jesus

Christ. An open mission field was in front of me, along with a divinely-appointed time to spread the Gospel.

Jonathan Woods was an arrogant and self-absorbed man. He was a straight 'A' college graduate; but unable to work cooperatively alongside anyone that wasn't as smart as him, resulting in contentious working conditions. His Electrical Engineering degree eventually proved worthless.

He later began selling insurance, working mostly on his own and doing well at it. He had the gift of gab, a good trait to have in a sales career.

"No one here is going to hell," he said, hoping to put the group at ease. "I know for a fact that when we die, that's it. Finito: Dust-to-dust and all of that stuff.

"Enjoy your life now because this could be your final day on the planet. And please don't forget that I've got excellent life-insurance packages to help those you leave behind."

Sid raised his hand and pointed to me. "Hey Eric, let's hear your answer. You've opened up a pretty good topic. What's your take on all of this?"

All eyes were on me. I wasn't used to such scrutiny with any of my opinions. How might I explain that someone invisible was leading me away from my old lifestyle; offering me a heavenly address, and healing my wounded soul?

I gave it my best shot. "In the past, I never put much emphasis on religion. However, I recently met a very dynamic lady, and a pretty one at that. She's given me much to think about regarding my eternal destiny."

"Anybody we know?" Gary asked with a devilish grin on his face. "And where did you meet her?"

"Her name is Marsha Kelly. And no, you wouldn't know her," I told him. "She lives in Detroit and rarely gets out this way. A few weeks back, I was at a local gas station when she drove in with a flat rear tire. I volunteered to change it and then invited her out to breakfast.

"She's a devout Christian on a mission to see souls saved. I told her not to waste her time with me. But thankfully, she kept on talking and shared the many wonderful things Jesus has done in her life."

The consensus among the group was unanimous. I was only listening to her with hopes of developing a relationship.

"What kind of person do you take me for?" I said, needing to set them straight. "For what it's worth, my heart was truly stirred. Marsha introduced me to Hope. She's very sincere about her convictions, and I look on that as a fine virtue for a woman to have."

My words fell on deaf ears. I wasn't too concerned about that, but was hopeful the conversation wouldn't end there.

"Keep telling yourself that and maybe you'll believe it," Bob suggested, glancing at the others with a nod and wink.

Sid asked if I was in love. I honestly wasn't sure. Saying those words out loud gave the matter new significance. To my surprise, admitting that I might be in love took some courage.

"Let's just say that, at this point, Marsha is the butter on my toast. She is my dream woman, and though I've not yet discussed any of this with her, she's tops in my eyes." That put an end to their sarcastic chatter.

Though I was a newcomer to faith in God, my heart, soul, and mind were in one accord. I knew for sure where I would be spending eternity.

The night ended with all of us talking more about the hereafter. That in itself was a telling miracle. An open door I didn't let slam shut.

7

My faults could fill a long list in anyone's book. With God's help, I've been attempting to improve myself. Being 54-years old now, two things I will say in my defense is that I've worked hard and always tried to do right by folks.

With my heart softened like a marshmallow the past few months, and my mind awakened to new insights from the Creator of the Universe, the brain in my head was on overload. All of these happenings were either something to brag about or keep to myself.

My long-time divorce continued haunting me. Who among us is without sin? Our intentions were right, but our actions ended up proving otherwise. In the beginning, I loved her more than I had ever loved any woman. Over the years, instead of falling deeper in love with each other, we fell out of love. And all we were left with was disappointment and heartbreak.

God's love is unconditional. What human being can say theirs is as well? How then could I be held accountable, yet I knew I would be. Who on this earth can love someone without a hint of selfishness? I can't, but should have tried to do better.

The thoughts in my head don't seem so sure about anything anymore. Have I blindly lived my life in spiritual darkness? Of course I did, up until now. I do recall catching an occasional glimpse of God's light, a match-head brightly burning for a few seconds and then dying out. And short-lived as that was, it gave me something to hope for.

The people I've most associated with throughout my life were probably as spiritually lost as me, or so it seemed. Quick hello's, fast goodbyes, foolish chatter, and shallow conversation were the norm.

Thankfully, a lady named Marsha Kelly came my way at the perfect time. She pointed me toward God. I needed help beyond my abilities. Life was not going my way, and I was treading water with weak arms. God was standing at the ready to reach down and pull me up. It took me far too long to call on Him, but thankfully I did.

I was sensing that God had plans for my life. Thinking as a business owner: Did He want me as an employee? As a spiritual infant how might I understand that? Was I expected to act as a mature biblical adult? That didn't seem possible at this point. However, throughout all of this, I could see God's hand moving in my everyday life.

In my heart-of-hearts I knew that my rock-solid business was ripe for selling. It had grown in value more than I imagined. Within a few weeks after listing it, a legitimate offer was made from an out-of-state concern. Six months of back and forth negotiations were needed to hammer out the hundreds of details.

Sitting with my accountant, two lawyers, and God's grace, the sale was finalized. I held no doubt that God oversaw each line and paragraph of the sale; from the final dollar amount to the protected positions and employees that were to remain working. When all the details were met to my satisfaction, I signed the papers.

Was my life over or just beginning anew? Preacher, teacher, candlestick maker, who was I kidding? Where was my faith?

"I'm headed in a new direction," I professed, with a slight quiver in my voice. My questioning friends, family, and associates couldn't easily accept what I was doing in leaving such a sure thing behind. Though I couldn't see the laughing demons of doubt, I did hear them. But only for a moment did they slow my steps.

The first day of retirement was rather uneventful. It was hard to believe, but for the first time in years, I had nowhere to go and nothing to do. A momentary fear overtook me. I was afraid of growing old and dying alone.

I took my time shaving and getting dressed before heading downstairs. While listening to the morning news on the radio, I shuffled around the kitchen preparing breakfast. No earth-shattering events had taken place. The sun was rising, birds were chirping, and the neighbor's dog, Oscar, barked his usual 'good morning'.

I seated myself at the table and bowed my head in prayer. "Dear Lord Jesus, thank you for your goodness. I am at your service. Please give me something to do with the rest of my life. Guide me and put your words into my heart. In your precious name, I pray. Amen."

A plateful of scrambled eggs, ham, and toast filled me up, along with four or five cups of coffee to wash it all down. That was it. Now what?

My thoughts were scattered. Would this turn out to be a day of mourning or jubilation? My heart was not yet tipping its hat. Was this going to be my new life?

I went about cleaning the kitchen, stopping for a moment to push open a window. An autumn breeze drifted in. I watched a noisy batch of rustling leaves flutter around the backyard. I felt nearly as wayward as some of them, standing slightly unsure of my direction in life. The days in front of me would be an unfolding story.

No circumstance seemed ordinary. When it rained, I thanked God for that. When I stubbed my toe, I asked God to forgive me for saying the wrong words.

Walking through my mind was the face of the person I most wanted to be with. I wondered how Marsha was doing.

Her twenty-five years of public school teaching was nearly at an end. Harsh cuts to the state's budget were leaving thousands of public employees with reduced benefits and wages. Many took a chance on positions outside of Michigan, and others were cornered into an early retirement.

Marsha responded to a posting for elementary teachers needed in Richmond, Virginia, and was invited down for a mid-summer interview. And regardless of the outcome, she made plans to stay a while longer and visit with a few of her old college friends.

With Marsha away, I wanted to spend more time focusing on God. From the many conversations I had with Him the past few months, I grew more appreciative of how great He is.

I wonder if God is flat-out bothered from hearing the same question, thousands of times over, from new believers like me: "Lord, what do you want me doing with my new life?" He is a patient God, for sure.

The silence was almost deafening. Something was wrong, and I'm sure it was on my end. I realized it was time to kneel and pray.

"Lord, please show me your plans for my life. I am at your service and ask for instructions. I confess to feeling lost when I don't hear from you. Forgive me for being impatient. Help me to trust you.

"Thank you for taking care of all my needs. I have money in the bank. I have good health. My heart is in your hands. Amen."

As one of the many billions of souls on Earth, should I always expect God to answer me? How many prayers from around the world is He hearing at the same time? My journey with Him would be a test of faith and patience.

One of the most important lessons I learned running a business was to pay my bills on time, if not sooner, and keep up with all of the other obligations. With God as my heavenly Master, being diligent in Christian responsibilities was going to be paramount. No easy task!

To make room for more of God in my heart, there were a few 'lingering items' that had to go. For a while, I wrongly believed preserving them in my heart was alright, and with no side effects. My own attempts at erasing them weren't successful. Removing those fingerprints required the Lord's help.

At one low-point in my life, I was blindsided by a woman who crashed into me like a powerful ocean wave, knocking me off my feet. Her happy ways lifted my spirit. Whenever she smiled at me, life felt better. We grew close to each other. I learned more from her than I want to admit. When we parted ways, I felt nearly dead. Thankfully, I recovered faster than I thought possible. But thoughts of her still linger.

Another entrenched memory was that of an older college student, who happened to work part-time in the same office as me. I fell for her like a ton of bricks. She nearly stopped my heart with her gorgeous dark eyes and all-knowing smile. We shared life together for six months. This was the woman I thought my life needed. A day with her was a heaven-sent prescription for the blues. Eventually she disappeared from my dreams, but not my heart.

Falling in love also goes beyond words. Music is part of that. I still remember the attractive girl in my seventh-grade class that I had a huge crush on. She was a big fan of The Beatles. Each time I heard them on the radio, I thought of her. Our family moved away that particular summer and I never saw her again. How sad I was to later learn of her early departure from life.

Memories anchoring me down to wishful-thinking and unpleasant regrets don't shine bright enough to want to go back to. Outside of my faith now, what is there left to chase after? God is making my life adventurous and exciting. He is all I want to follow after.

8

Marsha's red folder had been on my desk since I brought it home from our date. I was anxious to read through it, not knowing what I might find. She asked to know my thoughts when I was done.

I brewed a pot of coffee, grabbed the folder, settled down into my favorite recliner, and began reading. Right from the beginning her words resonated in my heart. I found myself relating to her soulful sentiments.

"Etched onto my soul is every scar, scrape, blister, and welt that I have suffered from stumbling through life's bloodstained valleys, and dragging myself over its broken rocks. But I believe the arduous journey has benefited me with an inner strength beyond my understanding.

"Though I have groaned and bellowed in agony, I am not alone. Hundreds-upon-hundreds of millions of wandering souls have been chased through similar valleys and dark, dank caves by the devil.

"Humanity will always be on the run from invisible enemies. But, are we left all alone in this world, heartlessly ignored by the very God who created us, to battle against the demons that aggravate and torment us?

"Absolutely not! There is an escape route. Yes, an honest-to-goodness path of deliverance to guide us through the valleys and straight back up to the mountain top. It sounds far too good to be true, I know.

"I have doubted and scoffed at that sort of thinking. Why wouldn't I? Life was not what I expected. Is it ever? Where did joy and peace scamper off to?

"Many believe disappointment and failure result from human imperfection; perhaps a type of punishment from impish gods for wrong behavior and selfish ambition. But even for the feeblest and most obstinate souls among us, there is hope.

"Is there a gift in heaven that can restore and revive humanity back to the condition God intended for us?

"The answer was already fixed in my heart: Salvation through Jesus Christ! So why did I continually fight hard against accepting it? The reason was foolish pride.

"In retrospect, I would have been better off seeking God sooner than I had. I needed a spiritual awakening in my life; one so majestically powerful that I would never forget it.

"My life was socially shallow. No new friends, no Prince Charming to date, and no hope for change in sight. Every day was the same for me. The sun came up and the sun went down. I needed a miracle in my life.

"But where on God's green earth are miracles to be found? Are they hiding in His pocket waiting to be tossed out like candy to hungry souls? I've often wondered if He gives miracles to nonbelievers.

"It was becoming difficult to tolerate such a humdrum

life. Year-after-year of doing the same things week-in and week-out, I knew there had to be something better. Where, oh where, was my miracle?

"Though I was unattached to the Miracle Giver, I didn't give up hope. I wanted gold but never went mining. Talk about wishful thinking. My pondering over life's precious secrets hidden from my eyes in no way means they don't exist: Hope among them.

"How in the world did reality end up squashing my dreams? It often seemed that it would be easier to give up 'fighting the fight' than to keep pressing on.

"My life wasn't a pretty picture. I blamed others for the disappointments and sorrows that bruised me through all the twists and turns of life. I fought brutally hard to get what I wanted, and came to the disparaging conclusion that life was mostly about survival of the fittest."

Marsha's emotional excursions were inspiring. Her transparency was refreshing. I felt the need to stand up and stretch, rub my eyes, and grab another cup of coffee.

It was one thing to sit across a dinner table from Marsha and chat, but to read the words that poured out of her heart onto paper was something else. What else would I learn about this incredible woman? I went back to reading.

"Thank you, Lord! Spring is only a moment away. The ground has thawed, and the last few stubborn mounds of snow have finally melted. Happy footsteps are taking over the landscape. Hidden smiles are being set free.

"Winter's reluctant goodbye wave ushers in renewed hope. A growing enthusiasm was lifting me, and countless other snowbound souls out of the winter doldrums. Dancing rays of sunlight thawed and warmed our frozen souls. I cherish these moments of joy and jubilation.

"Now for the bad news, the same problems I took into hibernation were still with me at winter's end. Life was speeding past me. There was no way I could catch up to it. And that train bound for glory had left me in the dust.

"The world continued changing without reason. Unsettling thoughts were dogging my every step. I was panicking. Was I the only one with this bad dream?

"I was a spry and energetic fifty-two-year-old woman, but could I outrun my disappointing past? No such luck. Running away wasn't the answer. Finally, the truth came out.

"Be who I'm supposed to be. How simple! What had it been, though, that kept me from becoming who I was meant to be? I zeroed in on the likeliest reasons: Wrong priorities, selfish goals, and hand-clapping trophies. My life had been nothing more than doing what others wanted of me.

"And just how does anyone know where to look for their inner-identity and answers to life's problems? I have wondered if asking too many deep questions will sink us into depression before there is time to find the answers. Sometimes it surely does seem that way.

"I've watched those around me flounder aimlessly searching for peace and tranquility. Their efforts always appeared futile. I wouldn't like going through any of that myself. I suppose my heart would have to be nearly obliterated before I ever smartened-up: Does God have the answers I've been looking for?

"Instead of looking inward, I took steps heavenward. The Bible clearly states that heaven is God's kingdom. Impressive!

"I've heard great things about heaven, yet it seems an awful lot of folks have differences of opinion about it."

I was pleasantly surprised at Marsha's insightful perceptions. Her words were touching my heart. And, in my eyes, the early steps of her Christian journey made her a more remarkable woman.

"Various philosophers see heaven as a fairy tale, a crutch for the emotionally hobbled; other spiritual dabblers describe heaven as nothing more than a 'Hall of Harps' where angels perform.

"During my younger years, I once had a curious vision of heaven that went beyond angels and harps to a spacious banquet room filled with divine delicacies. I had no basis for such an imaginative occurrence.

"I took hold of a beautiful plate and moved fast. I was desperate to find a serving bowl filled with new dreams. Maybe too, I'd find a bowl of precious hope and sweet joy. One spoonful of that liquid gold would surely nourish my hungry soul. A slice of heavenly bread and a portion of rich-tasting meat would have been exquisite. But before I could sit down and eat, my time there ran out.

"The Bible, so to speak, hands us God's perfect truth on a silver platter. Even after surrendering my life to Jesus Christ, I need much more time to straighten out my wrong-thinking about Him. Heaven truly is God's Holy residence.

"Many of the people and pleasures I thought were so important in life, proved utterly worthless. My insatiable and worldly desires kept me running in circles.

"How many men and women have been tripped up looking for someone to love? My own path is well littered.

"It does ring true that we learn many tough lessons

through our sufferings. I remember the names of men who led me on, then cruelly left me bleeding and dangling over shark-infested waters, unconcerned whether I made it back to safety. Well, too bad for them. I'm still here. They'll get their due reward some day.

"I ask myself, where do I go once my feet are back on solid ground, and what compass do I use for directions? The Bible eventually became my moral compass, directing me to God's path."

A quick distraction tickled me. For a moment, I thought I heard Marsha whispering, word for word, what I was reading from her folder. There was something funny about that. The woman seems stuck in my head.

"From time to time, in earlier years, my mind played unkind games on me. Whenever the sun was shining bright, I immediately went to wondering how soon before rain clouds moved in. I hated when that happened.

"And whenever my heart might be singing a happy tune because I had fallen in love, that's when I would sadly discover that love isn't all it's cracked up to be.

"From uncaring people to mean-spirited intruders dirtying the floor of my heart, I was regularly in a state of brokenness. Each night in bed, I rolled, tossed, turned, and incessantly wondered: Why me? How dare they? Etc., etc., etc.

"Many friends have come and gone in my life. Yet I still know of a few wonderful human angels close by, hovering over me during the harsh storms of life. I refer to them as my Redwoods, beautiful, deep-rooted, loyal, strong, tall, and true."

Marsha's pages were done. I felt sad. Not one more to

be read. She didn't know it, but my thoughts and emotions were nearly identical to hers.

Amazing! That's the word I breathed out. I hoped Marsha would write more. Yet all of what she had just given me was definitely going to provide a mountain of things for us to talk about.

9

Donovan Steele was a tall man with a ruddy complexion, neatly sporting a few tufts of gray in his brown hair. It had been fifteen years since we had last seen each other. For the next few days, he would be a guest in my home.

I picked him up from Detroit's Metro Airport. From there, we headed to a good restaurant for dinner. There was an odd look about him that was difficult to describe. He looked a little on the frail side, and I detected a hint of restrained chaos peeking out from behind his easy-to-spot forced smiles.

The restaurant was busy. As we waited for menus, Donovan asked how life had been treating me. "Pretty well," I answered, not wanting to go into a lot of detail. "And how are things for you and Mrs. Steele?"

"Life has been good to me, but not all of it," he said, almost whispering. A sad look messed up his face.

Whatever difficulties had crossed his path was not easy for him to talk about. I knew enough to leave the matter alone. I noticed a small tattoo of a Cross on the inside of Donovan's left wrist, and asked how it came to be.

"Oh that," he remarked. "Before my wife and I were married, she was quite the active Christian. As a symbol of our love for each other, she wanted both of us to have a Cross tattooed on our wrist." As he finished talking, tears slipped down his face.

In stunned silence, I prayed, "Lord, please comfort Donovan's heart. Help him to feel peace."

A long moment later, he spoke through a broken voice. "I'm sorry, Eric. It's hard to control my emotions right now. I'm hurting bad."

"Don't worry," I said. "Let's head over to my place." Twenty minutes later we were sitting in my living room. Donovan was mostly quiet.

I wanted him to have a few minutes of privacy, hoping it might calm him down. I excused myself, walking over to the kitchen to brew a pot of coffee. Returning back, I found him on the edge of the couch, both hands covering his face. He was moaning.

Donovan fell to the floor with a thud. On his hands and knees, he cried out. "I need help! Someone, please help me. I can't stop drinking."

I'd never seen or heard a man cry so hard, and from so deep within. I moved down alongside him, slipping my arm over his shoulders.

"Jesus will help you. He's helped me and can help you." Though my words may have sounded like an impossible promise, I had to be strong for Donovan. I didn't leave his side.

He grabbed onto my arm for a steady brace back up to the couch. With a quivering voice, he let out all the hurt buried inside him.

"Rebecca Lynn Steele, my wife of ten years, walked away with our two children. She left me at my lowest point. I could barely function. I felt as though my soul were dying. There seemed no reason to live. I had lost my job, and there was no money left in our bank account. No one would hire me.

"She put up with my drinking and abuse for more than a year, then left me cold without so much as a hug. I heard the door close. She drove away and never returned."

I was desperate to help my friend. "Lord, I don't know what to do. Donovan is falling apart right before my eyes."

Though we had rarely kept in touch over the years, he and I shared similar interests. We attended the same high school, had mutual friends, and took classes together in community college.

He was looking to make his way in the world, and headed south to Roanoke, Virginia, taking a sales position with a major automotive supplier. He worked hard building up a clientele, eventually becoming the top salesman for their east coast and Midwest territories.

Near the height of his career, he met and fell in love with Rebecca Lynn Waters. She managed the steakhouse where he occasionally dined. It wasn't long before they started dating, and six months later he asked for her hand in marriage.

Donovan was regularly earning sizeable bonuses. The more success he gained, the more time he spent in countless pubs and bars pandering to new customers. He was taking in large amounts of alcohol, and for a short while never saw it as a problem.

Soon enough though, his drinking grew into a difficult

matter. Not only was his marriage being hurt, but his largest customers began missing timely orders and receiving incorrect invoices.

The main office pulled Donovan off the road. He couldn't defend his mistakes and was given stern warnings. The problems remained. He was fired.

The booze he was drowning in cost him his job and marriage. Rebecca was unable to pull her husband out of his rut. She ran out of patience and filed for divorce.

Donovan had only a few distant friends, and little hope left. His bad circumstances grew mountainous. His court-ordered child support payments could not be met, ending visitations with his children.

His drinking drained him of every bit of dignity and self-worth. Most nights he sat crying in the busted-down flat he barely could afford. A few manual-labor jobs were his only means of income.

Donovan was no longer applauded, honored, and heralded. He hit bottom, staggering about woefully alone as if dragging an anchor.

There was no hope for souls like him and never would be; at least that's what the devil kept shouting in his ear. He finally believed it.

More than once, he hunted for any nasty substance to end his life with. His pockets were usually empty, and even the local drug pushers wanted nothing to do with him. He had become just another broken human being lying face down in the wretched-gutters of life. The world had turned its back on him.

Then, miraculously, inside the pocket of an old duffel bag he had hung onto from the divorce, Donovan discovered four, $100 bills along with a handful of jeweled trinkets awarded him for topping company sales. Finding his way to the closest pawn shop, he sold off the varied pieces.

Donovan finally had enough money to purchase a one-way plane ticket to Michigan, and also pay the extra postage to send a registered letter to Eric.

He hoped he was escaping from the valley of broken dreams; the love of his life, the children they made, the success he enjoyed, and the hellish ruin of it all.

Donovan left Virginia on a wing and a prayer. He would have one more opportunity to experience God's merciful love; free to those who had perhaps once known Him, and those who never did.

10

I was one who preferred to stop and study what was going on around him. But as God was now actively directing my life, the luxury of relaxed thought was greatly diminished.

My life had been changing faster than I imagined possible. In only a handful of weeks, I became a follower of Jesus Christ, sold my business, and began telling others how Jesus changed my life. Every day was now a blessing, not a burden. Holy Scripture was becoming food for my soul.

The dilemma in all of this was a curious one. There wasn't an ounce of salesmanship within me. I didn't see myself as a preacher. How could I sell others on Jesus Christ? At best, my word skills were only average. Most every quality a preacher needs, I do not possess.

I recalled Marsha's prophetic words. "God was going to open doors for me to tell others about His free gift of salvation through Jesus Christ."

Yes, I was a believer now, but could I become a mouthpiece for Him? I've read in the Bible how God uses the weak to confound the strong and foolish things of the world to confound the wise.

Was I being disobedient in denying His call to tell others the Good News? The way I saw it, my skill set was in different areas. I built a business from the ground up. I could find some amount of good in a pile of rubble, and knew that a rundown building could be fixed up. I knew how to put a business plan together convincing a bank to lend me money.

My mind made a quick connection to something. Jesus can find good in a discarded soul, heartlessly pitched out on a garbage heap. He can rebuild anyone willing to let Him. I know.

But this matter of telling others about our Savior, well, I had no idea how to do that. There was no logical reason as to why a man like me would be given a divine assignment. Others are far more qualified, and there certainly is no halo floating over my head, nor any Bible school diploma hanging on my wall.

How many of my close friends and acquaintances need to hear of God's love; more than I want to admit. In hopes of convincing others of God's greatness, I must learn more about His love and power to deliver.

I asked God why He would allow me to share the Gospel. His answer made perfect sense. Who better to tell others about the free gift of salvation, than someone who has already been saved?

My next question must have sounded foolish. Where did I find the courage to even ask it?

"Lord, are you sure you want me? How can I share your free gift of salvation with anyone as cynical and skeptical as I used to be? Even as a believer, my words will surely seem questionable and not believable."

As for me, walking with God is becoming a step-by-step and life-long journey. No shortcuts whatsoever can be taken.

Thinking back on the steps I took towards God, He mercifully accepted me just as I was. I don't recall Him telling me to stop and clean up my life. Yet, in no way was that a pass to remain living a sinful life.

The morning we first met and shared breakfast together, I remember Marsha talking about God's loyalty to His children. "Jesus continues helping me overcome sin," she said.

I believed her. And why wouldn't I? God has been helping me in the same way. A sincere prayer escaped from my lips. "Oh Lord, allow me to hang onto your hand and please lead me wherever you will. Please help me turn my life away from sin. Take control of my life. Amen."

What I heard next was almost heart-stopping! In only a few seconds and less than twenty words, God spoke a lifetime of instruction to me.

"Follow me, trust me, obey me, and lean not on your understanding." Those words were a precious gift from God. I hid them in my heart.

Of all the gurus and self-help voices in the world, I knew that God in heaven was the only one who could take my life and do something miraculous with it.

From moment-to-moment, I love how God keeps surprising me. Rising from bed two days after Donovan Steele suffered his emotional breakdown in my living room, an unusual thought tickled my heart, and I laughed out loud at it. More than once, showering that morning, I asked God if I was hearing Him right.

He wanted me looking my best that morning at the breakfast table. I wasn't sure what my dressing up would accomplish, but my obedience to God is most important. Would I automatically ever come to do that?

Donovan Steele was a marked man. In his own eyes he was a failure. His children no longer had their father; his former wife wanted nothing at all to do with him. Howling winds of death encircled him, extinguishing the last flickering flame of hope in his soul.

I entered the kitchen offering up a casual "good morning" to Donovan. The person slouched at my table was probably feeling as bad as he looked; groggy, unshaven, and pajama clad. The strained look on his face revealed his weakened condition.

Donovan couldn't see beyond his suffering soul. How could he? All he could feel were gnawing pains in every part of his body. But in catching sight of me, Donovan jumped up in surprise. "You look amazing! Is this how you dress first thing in the morning? Do you have a funeral or something special to attend?"

I didn't tell him it was God who instructed me to put on the suit. I had no clue as to what God had in store for Donovan. Two days earlier, he was a desperate man crying on my living room floor, begging for a fresh start to his broken life.

Right in front of him now was someone saying that hope was available. "Do you want a new life?" I asked. "If you really do, I know someone who will take you by the hand and walk you through to victory." The pained and disinterested look on his face spoke volumes to me.

Jesus obviously was not an unfamiliar name in Donovan's life. Even though the small Cross tattooed on his wrist did not influence his lifestyle, it apparently set off a raging spiritual battle between his heart and soul.

A day earlier, Donovan complained to me about his ex-wife, saying that she would plead with him to attend church and pray with her, and wisely become a Godly example for their children. She practiced what she preached, but he rarely gave lip-service to her requests.

Donovan got up from the breakfast table, and with shaky hands, pushed back his hair and straightened his pajamas. "My friend, from the bottom of my heart, I thank you," he said, as a few tears momentarily filled his eyes.

"You've been kind and gracious to me the past few days, and I commend you for being so helpful. But you're not the same Eric Matthews I remember. It seems you've become a serious-minded man. Thinking back, do you recall the stupid things we did in the name of enjoying life, and how much we used to party in high school and college?"

I couldn't make any excuses for such behavior. My memory brought back plenty of guilt and regrets.

"What I'd rather do is forget how foolish and immature we were," I said. "The most important thing for us is to find ways to improve ourselves with wise choices and right thinking. We're on similar paths. You need a miracle, and I very recently received one. That is an amazing circumstance!

"Here we are at my kitchen table, right where God wants us. We need to open our hearts to the Creator of the Universe and listen to His Words."

Donovan watched in earnest as I folded my hands together and prayed.

"Lord, we place our needs before you, asking for wisdom, guidance, and favor. The miracles we need are ones only you can provide. Donovan needs deliverance from alcohol. He needs his marriage and family restored. He needs a purpose in life and meaningful employment. Bless us with your peace and direction, as we walk day-by-day on the path you set before us. Amen."

11

I could only wonder how things got so bad for Donovan. Had he ever sought professional help? I couldn't beat around the bush anymore. A mound of concerns surfaced in my thoughts. In the entire matter of wanting to see a hurting friend get back to a productive life, I was fully aware of my inability to help him.

Donovan sat back down at the kitchen table, finishing up the last of his coffee. I spoke to him as a brother. "I know your heart is hurting. The best thing I can do is re-introduce you to the One who will meet your needs and heal your broken heart."

For some reason my words must have riled him. Donovan suddenly became defensive. His face grew red, giving way to an inner-rage about to explode, a true alcoholic's temper. I saw him clench his fists. He was about to come apart, but not before speaking his mind.

"I know who you're talking about," he said, nearly shouting. "I don't think Jesus is too concerned about helping me. We had a few encounters, but I walked away to show Him just what I thought of His unfair demands. So don't give me the Jesus routine, okay? I've heard it all before. I'm sick of it. That isn't why I came to you.

"I only showed up here to ask for a job. It's intimidating to be sitting around here in my pajamas, while you're dressed in a suit and tie. You're the one with the big business and fine reputation. Can you help me with a job? Surely there is something you can hire me for. Please, anything."

Donovan needed to hear the truth. "Knock off the anger!" I said, getting loud. "You couldn't have known this, but I'm retired now. I sold my business a month ago. But if you'll allow me, I will pray with you and lead you to Jesus. Don't take it out on me if you're mad at Him. You need His help."

The last bit of resolve Donovan possessed was gone. Being without alcohol was taking a hard toll on him. He had been through it before attempting to wean himself dry, but couldn't. He was sick and tired of being out of control. Even I could see that.

Live or die, Donovan wanted to get fall-down drunk. He was mad at the world, ready to point a finger of blame at every face that moved through his memory. With the only honest friend he had left in the world standing in front of him, Donovan became enraged with a fit of jealous anger. He couldn't hold back.

"Jesus doesn't want anything to do with me," Donovan shouted through his pain. "Can't you see that? He doesn't take people like me back. I'm a dead man. What can I do for Him?"

His hurting words surprised me. I answered him back with honesty and love. "That's a terrible lie from the devil!

Jesus took me back and will do the same for you. He's no respecter of persons."

What I saw next frightened me. Donovan began shaking. Beads of sweat covered his face as the muscles in his legs and back were stiffening. His head dropped down over his folded arms.

Gasps of pain were making their way out of his throat. He couldn't control the unrelenting spasms of pain randomly shooting through his body. I hurried to a hall closet and came back with a blanket to wrap around him. He was in a death lock.

I still carried with me the phone number of an area substance abuse center that helped one of my former employees. With Donovan's permission, I called them. An hour later their transport van pulled into my driveway. I signed their forms accepting total financial responsibility for Donovan's treatment, and then followed them over to the Center. I was informed by the attending doctor, that it could be two months before Donovan was released.

On my drive home, I heard from God. "I want you to visit Donovan once a week. Hurt and guilt have been crushing his soul. Pain and anger have derailed his mind. I am cleaning up all the damage in him.

"And just like what was around your heart, there is a deadening crust around his too. My hands will carefully remove it. Be quick and generous in sending money to Rebecca for the children. You have more than enough in the bank for that."

12

A serene calmness followed me around the house as I went room-to-room cleaning and straightening up. It had only been a couple of days since Donovan's admittance into rehab. As much as I enjoyed the peace and quiet, nipping at my heels was a deep-feeling of ineptness at living a life of faith.

God reminded me of His instructions. "Follow, trust, obey, and do not lean on your understanding."

Inept or not, I was ready to take on the assignment He had just given me concerning Rebecca.

My first visit with Donovan was a surprisingly candid one "What a fool I was to think I could beat the devil," he said, looking straight at me. His eyes were still bloodshot, and a hint of Jaundice had tainted his skin.

"I thought I could overcome my drinking. For me to invade your home and put you smack dab in the middle of my problems was wrong. Please forgive me."

"Don't worry about that," I remarked. "We'll get through this together. Right now, I need Rebecca's contact information. It's only right she knows you're here. I'll get in touch with her later.

"There is something more God wants me to do on your behalf."

"What's that?" Donovan asked, sounding concerned.

"Send money for her and the children," I answered. "And once you're out of here, we'll discuss how to get you back in good standing with the Friend-of-the-Court, and hopefully back together with Rebecca."

Hearing even the slimmest possibility of reconciling with his family injected sizzling hot drops of hope back into Donovan's heart.

He asked me to pray with him, an encouraging sign for sure. "I want back those things I've lost; my wife, family, job, and my sanity. Is God aware of what I'm going through?"

"Of course He is!" I told him, ready and willing to pray. "Dear Lord, please watch over Donovan and relieve him of the pain in his body and the anguish in his soul. Cover him with your peace from top to bottom. Let him sense your presence while he recovers in this place. Restore him back to a wholesome life. Thank you, Jesus. Amen."

As we hugged goodbye, I promised to be back within the week. I headed home to call Rebecca. Would she care about Donovan's condition? Was there any possibility of reconciliation in her heart?

Might she remember me well enough to discuss the events of the last few weeks? The last time we had spoken was soon after their first child was born.

Rebecca voiced no surprise over the news that Donovan was now in rehab. Regarding talk of reconciliation, her response was stern and cold-hearted; in that she was presently dating a man she believed was perfect for her and the children.

"There is no going back to someone like Donovan," she grumbled. "He went beyond destroying our family; he destroyed himself. Once we were divorced there was only one thought on my mind; cut my losses and run.

"Do you really expect me to welcome him home? He's a loser. How would our children deal with him moving back in with us? They saw the devastation he caused. No sir. I'm not going to put myself or the children through any more of his problems."

I understood her thinking, but was disappointed. I hoped she might still have had some amount of compassion and concern for him.

The court tabulated the money Donovan owed for unpaid child support. I immediately sent them a check to bring his account up to date, adding in three additional payments.

By week's end, I was praying for my next God-given assignment. Moment-by-moment, I sensed myself moving into deeper waters with Jesus Christ. That was a far cry from my old lifestyle, wanting always to be sure-footed and on dry ground.

The years I lived without Christ was like having one-hand tied behind my back. I relied on my own thoughts and wisdom to determine what ingredients were necessary for success. Was it having lots of money and power, perhaps even fame?

A clear answer from 1st Timothy 6: 10, (New International Version) gave me the right advice: "For the love of money is a root of all kinds of evil."

Retraining my thoughts regarding money would take time. But now as a Christian, I could at least ask for His help. I certainly wasn't going to argue with God, who also told us to flee from seeking riches; and instead pursue righteousness, godliness, faith, love, endurance, and gentleness.

What about God's true riches? I looked it up. Proverbs 3: 13-14, "Blessed are those who find wisdom, those who gain understanding, for she is more profitable than silver and yields better returns than gold."

Could I handle more instruction? Proverbs 3: 5-6, "Trust in the Lord with all your heart and lean not on your own understanding; in all your ways submit to Him, and He will make your paths straight."

All I had to do now was obey these priceless nuggets of truth, given to us straight from God's heart.

13

Within 24-hours, two unexpected phone calls brought me a quick surge of anxious energy. Was God sending more surprises my way?

Marsha Kelly needed a ride home from the airport the following Friday. Her month-long stay in Virginia was coming to an end. Nothing would make me happier than to see her again.

I spotted her coming out of the airport with luggage in hand. I called out her name. She looked wonderful. Her hair was stylishly shorter, and she had a nice tan.

Minutes later, we were driving on the freeway. "Did you have a nice flight in?" I asked.

"It was good," she said, sounding tired. "For me, it's those glittering city lights that is the icing on the cake. That's why I always ask for a window seat.

"And Eric, before I forget, thank you for coming out and driving me home at this late hour." She was always quick with a thank you.

"No problem, glad I could be of help."

I wanted to know how things turned out with her interview. Was she moving to Virginia?

"Well, they wanted to hire me for a sixth-grade class teaching English literature and composition," Marsha said. "I told them I would need a few days to think it all through.

"I seriously wanted to accept their offer. The salary was much more than I expected. The location was nice, and a good number of apartments were available for rent. Yet something about the matter wasn't right.

"I couldn't put my finger on it, but there was a signal from my heart to proceed with caution. I was diligent in seeking the Lord about it. He was silent. If I turned it down though, I would come home wondering if I was replaced."

"What did you decide?"

"I had to say no," she answered, letting out a sigh of frustration. "If teaching is no longer His plan for me, what else am I qualified for? All of these obstacles mean only one thing; it's time for me to fast and pray. Just before His arrest in the Garden of Gethsemane, Jesus prayed these words, "Father, not my will, but yours be done."

In a soft voice, Marsha spoke those same words, "Father, not my will, but yours be done."

Parking curbside in front of Marsha's house, I carried her luggage to the front door and asked if we could meet for lunch one day. I wanted to fill her in on all the Lord had been doing in my life.

"Give me time to get settled," she said, flashing a last-second smile. "I promise to call you and set something up."

I wanted God's permission to remain in contact with Marsha. "Lord, she has touched my heart and soul. Would you have any objections to me pursuing a serious relationship with her? A woman that amazing isn't somebody I want to pass up."

As I got ready for bed that evening, I took a moment to pray for Marsha. "Lord, may she hear from you on where to teach. Open the right door for her. Amen"

Was her faith being tested? "That might be," she said to me later. But this was a timely matter for her. Without fully knowing what to do, she couldn't accept their offer.

She never knew God to be cruel. He had always been her provider, nurturer, and protector. This was new territory for her.

Unbeknownst to me, Marsha was at home praying too. All of the job offer concerns fell by the wayside. Her heart was suffering from loneliness. And wouldn't it finally be something, she thought, if God would take care of that.

From experience, she knew it was always best to be forthright in prayer. "Jesus, I've gazed at the stars and marvel at your wondrous creation. But God, I'm lonely and ask to meet the man you've prepared for me. Is there a man somewhere who won't judge me by my flaws, and who will allow me to see what his are; so that we can possibly get better together?

"I've reached middle age. I don't want to be with anyone you don't approve of, and I don't want to be unequally yoked. Is Eric the man for me? Should I entertain any further thoughts about him?

"He is different than any other I've met, and I feel comfortable with him. You've always protected me. You've guided me through valleys and the dark storms of life. I ask for your help in this next stage of my life.

"It seems that on this issue of my personal happiness, you've been awfully quiet. If I'm spiritually married to you, ought I even be thinking about marriage to a man? Don't let me become impatient or angry with you."

Marsha couldn't bring herself to be mad at God. She would have to be totally out of her mind to be angry with the Holy One who saved her soul and paid the penalty of her sins.

14

Sid Jackson took a deep breath as he phoned Eric. A serious matter needed to be discussed, forcing him to speak from his heart. Not an easy thing for Sid.

It had always been his contention that those wearing their heart on their sleeve were just plain weak. Real men don't cry, and real men never let on that they're hurting. Sid practiced what he preached.

But, as often happens in life, regrets and stressful situations began piling up. Not surprisingly, Sid's heart was beginning to change.

He started the phone conversation talking about our upcoming gathering. Since I would be hosting the event, Sid asked if everything was good-to-go on my end.

"No problem," I said. "I've got plenty of fine grilling meat and am looking forward to a fun night. We might even have time for another round of 'guy talk'. Think you're up for that?"

"Oh, absolutely," he said. "And since you brought it up, how about the two of us get a head start? You're the only honest-to-goodness Christian I know, and I've got questions for you." I was struck by his receptive attitude.

"Come over tomorrow at three o'clock," I suggested. "Don't forget, I'm a new Christian and no expert. But I'll do my best to answer your questions."

Sid Jackson had all the advantages of being born into a very wealthy family. He, his two brothers and two sisters were raised by parents who trusted in their wealth. No need for faith, no need for crying about anything. Money was their god.

Each fateful twist and turn of Sid's adult life took a heavy toll on him. Being twice married and divorced cut deeply into his heart. Even with all of the money he possessed, he admitted that his failures could not be erased.

Ministering directly with Sid, or anyone else for that matter, would be a new experience for me. I wanted our discussion to be enlightening, and I prayed for wisdom.

"Thank you for having me over," Sid remarked, entering the house.

"So, what's on your mind?" I asked, not sure of all his concerns.

"Well, more than anything, I'm wondering about you becoming a Christian," he stated. "You seriously caught us all off guard last month. Since then, I've been trying to deal with your question.

"Not ever being a religious person, I hadn't actually given it much thought. Where will I spend eternity when I die? That's a pretty powerful thing to be asked."

"You're definitely not alone on that," I told him. "I'm sure most people, if they're honest, will admit they don't spend much time thinking about their eternal destiny. I rarely did myself."

A good hour later, after we had discussed salvation and forgiveness, Sid confessed that he was still unsure about becoming a follower of Christ. He asked if that really mattered to God, and could he put off making a decision.

"I strongly suggest not delaying your decision," I cautioned him. "2nd Corinthians 6: 2 states that now is the time of God's favor, and now is the day of salvation.

"Sid, if you fell over dead right now, without Jesus in your heart you'd be barred from entering heaven.

"And yes, becoming a follower of Christ is of the utmost importance to God. For some, accepting Jesus Christ as their Savior is an easy decision. Others struggle with personal guilt over the vileness of their sins and the shame of owning up to them. They put off deciding because they don't believe they're good enough, or that God would never forgive them. Some people even flat-out refuse to believe in God."

Sid's face tightened. My answers must have hit a nerve. He was glaring intently into my eyes, wanting only the truth. No beating around the bush, just honest answers.

"You hit the nail on the head," he responded. "That's what I've been struggling with. If there were some way I could know for sure that God would forgive all the sins I've committed throughout my life, I would jump at the chance to become a believer.

"Eric, you've known me for decades and the sort of person I am. I've done more than my fair share of sinning, and I'm not proud about that. Being rich, I suppose, made me think I wasn't responsible for my behavior, as if my mistakes weren't really sins, but only foolish behavior."

Throughout all the years of our friendship, I had never seen a more serious look on Sid's face.

"Can a guy like me be forgiven?" He asked with a hopeful breath.

"Yes!" I answered. "A guy like you can be forgiven. And I tell you that because God forgave me. He's no respecter of persons. So whether it's a downright nasty sin or a little white lie, sin is sin."

In one quick motion, Sid Jackson leaped up from the couch. "I'm ready for this!" He shouted. "I am ready! Will you help me? What do I do now? What do I say?" I was overwhelmed by the man standing in front of me, and truly surprised by his enthusiastic reaction.

"Oh my Lord God in heaven," I thought. If Sid was ready, I was just as ready to jump and shout for joy with him.

"Sid, listen and repeat after me. Mean these words from your heart: "Lord Jesus, I call upon your name and ask to be saved. Forgive me of all of my sins. Come into my heart and help me to live for you every single day of my life. I receive your free gift of salvation. Thank you, Jesus! Amen."

I reached over and gave him a tight embrace, stating that we'd just become brothers in the Lord! "For all eternity, we will be part of the same family."

Sid's face was radiant. "I'm so overwhelmed right now; I'm just about to fall over!" He yelled out. "This is not at all how I expected to feel.

"I am forgiven! Thank you, Jesus! Thank you! Thank you! Thank you!"

Sid wasn't holding back, and why would he, especially

after his heart was close to exploding with invisible joy? Standing straight and with both arms stretched skyward, Sid's face beamed with joy as tears of happiness glistened on his face.

How does a rescued man thank those who pulled him out of cold, swirling waters? Both of us shared the jubilant moment. I was shouting praises too. Time seemed to have disappeared. Eventually, a quiet calm overcame us. A stabilizing air of tranquility filled the room.

"Eric, I don't even know how to say thank you. Whatever just happened here, well, I'm beyond understanding any of it. Except for this one thing: God has touched my heart, and I have a new life to start living."

The following week we had plans to be in the very same room together. Other friends would be with us, and who could say what might take place during that gathering.

15

I was in bed when the phone rang. It was the morning after Sid Jackson's moment of salvation. An unfamiliar voice startled me.

"This is Dr. William Schaffer from The Morrison Rehabilitation Center. May I speak with Eric Matthews?"

"This is him." A sudden feeling of dread hit me. "Is something wrong?" I asked, still half-asleep.

"I'm sorry to have to tell you this," he said, "but Donovan Steele passed away an hour ago. How soon can you be here?"

The doctor's words didn't register. I froze up. My mind went numb. In a hurried swirl of motion, I dressed and rushed out the door.

"No, this can't be true," I mumbled, driving with both hands tight on the steering wheel. "Lord, they must be wrong. It's got to be a mistake. This just can't be." All of my senses were dulled with shock, anger, and confusion.

The moment I arrived at the center, I was escorted to Dr. Schaffer's office.

"Please, have a seat. I'm as dumbfounded as you probably are right now." The doctor's words gave me no comfort.

"I've seen this happen on rare occasions," he said, pointing out how quickly an unexpected death could occur with an addicted patient. "The autopsy will give us the answers."

I was mad at an invisible force. Mad at the wind. "It was only a few days ago that I was here," I said. "Donovan looked stable and was talking clearly. What could have gone wrong so fast?"

As Donovan had no siblings and his parents were deceased, the doctor asked if I would identify the body. The finality of his death shoved a dagger of sharp sorrow through my heart. I let out a deep wail of sadness upon seeing his corpse.

The doctor gave me access to a private office. I was alone with myself. The tears I had not yet cried that morning were coming down hard.

Nothing was making sense. My thoughts were out of control and dragging me through dark valleys I had long forgotten about.

Could Donovan's death have been my fault? Was there something I didn't do in trying to help him? I went back to remembering the previous night's joy over Sid Jackson's spiritual conversion. But in the blink of an eye, that joy was devoured by the tragic reality of a man who slipped down an all-too-familiar mountain – the one that glitters but isn't gold.

Two phone calls were waiting to be made. I needed advice from my lawyer on matters pertaining to Donovan's passing. And then, since I was the last person he resided with, though only for a few days, the police would need additional information regarding Donovan for their report.

The other call was to Rebecca Steele, which ended up on her phone message recording. Without giving the sad details, I asked her to call back as soon as possible.

An anxious prayer came out of my mouth: "Father God, help me and any others who might be heartbroken over this man's death. Take control of everything that needs your touch. Thank you for your mercy. Amen."

Why is life so unpredictable? There are no easy answers to that question. Death is somehow related to eternity. Never again will that person's life reside on earth. There's no coming back to the family they were part of.

An enormous mountain of mystery rose in front of me; I couldn't see a way around it. My sorrow-filled thoughts were confused. Are life and death all we should concern ourselves with? Had I forgotten about God? He knows all the answers.

I wanted to run and hide somewhere far away. Instead, I kneeled and prayed. "God, please give me something I can grab hold of. I'm under a blanket of darkness. Let me see your Light.

"Your Word says that when I am weak you will make me strong. I ask for strength in my bones, my spirit, my soul, my heart."

I dared not think about the possibility of my friend going to hell. I stood back up, wondering if Donovan was in heaven singing with the angels. Did he open his heart to Jesus before taking his last breath?

All of a sudden, I lost touch with reality. Angry questions bellowed out of me. I threw them at God. "How could you? What kind of God are you?"

I remained yelling. Immediately I realized that was the wrong thing to do. Everything next happened so fast. A heavy curtain of icy fear engulfed me. This had to be the devil looking for a way to try and beat the faith out of me.

I didn't see any of it coming. A condemning slap of shame cracked across my face, while stinging bullets of doubt and guilt tore through my flesh. A hard, steel-fisted punch to the gut doubled me over, crumbling me to my knees. Then a brutal and blinding kick to my head nearly finished me off.

The deep and harsh-sounding groans coming out of my throat would have frightened any bystander. "Oh God, Oh God, Oh God." I didn't move. I couldn't move.

My face was painfully sore. Both eyes were closed tight and burning in a river of salty tears. Would I ever know peace? Minutes passed before the hurting started to subside.

"Lord," I cried out, as my mouth slowly began working. "You created us. You know the calendar of our life. You do as you see fit. I can't hide my tears. You know my thoughts. Is Donovan in heaven?"

Incredibly, and in the blink of an eye, a bright moment of clarity bubbled across my brain. It stirred and awakened me. Amazingly, as though nothing had just happened, I rose, breathed deep, and felt alive. I coughed and swallowed, stretched out my arms, flexed my fingers, and opened my eyes.

The only thought I had was to get home. I stepped out into the hallway and headed towards the lobby. Passing by the receptionist, I told her I was going home and to call me if I was needed.

I spent the rest of that afternoon and evening face-down on the living room couch. Every thought in my head was one of dark disbelief. There wasn't a moment of peace in my soul.

At one point, I remember answering the phone. It was Rebecca Steele calling back.

"Did something happen to Donovan?" Sadness kept me from answering. Several seconds passed before I could speak.

"Oh, dear Rebecca, this is hard to tell you. Donovan passed away this morning."

Was she going to cry? She didn't. Her words were respectful, but not sad.

"I'm sorry to hear that," she said flatly. "Send me whatever details you can about his burial, etc. I'll speak to the children tomorrow about his passing. Thank you for calling me."

For news so tragic, the phone call was short. It was nearly midnight when I got into bed.

With my head on the pillow, the sadness of the day attacked me once more, from Dr. Schaffer's morning call, the horror of death, my torturous despair, and the demanding expectations of faith.

Pulling the covers over me, I wanted to be hard asleep and nearly was when the phone rang.

"Please, Lord, no more bad news."

"Marsha?"

"Yes. Hi."

"Is everything alright?" I asked.

"Everything is fine," she said. "I hoped we could talk."

Dear sweet Marsha. Her voice was like sugar. As awful as I was feeling, the voice of that precious angel speaking into my ear was close to heaven.

"Have you been busy these past few days?" She questioned.

Top to bottom and inside out, I was a mess. My emotions were raw. I didn't know how to answer her.

I wanted more of this woman in my life, but over the few months we had known each other; our visits rarely went beyond light-hearted conversation and me listening to her wonderful and much needed biblical guidance. She was beyond my emotional understanding. I wanted to reach her with my heart. But for now, that would have to wait.

"Marsha, this day has been awful," I finally shared. "Donovan Steele, an old friend of mine, came up to see me a few weeks ago from Virginia. I invited him to stay here in my home. He was down on his luck after he and his wife divorced. He was a heavy drinker. He was not allowed to see his children.

"His job was gone, and so was his hope and dignity. I was praying that I could somehow help him. Within a few days here, he suffered a physical breakdown. I was able to get him admitted to a rehab clinic. This morning they called me and said he died overnight."

Upon hearing my sadness, Marsha didn't ask any questions. The silence was awkward. I had to speak.

"I don't understand him dying so suddenly. This whole ordeal has me in a dark corner of doubt. Donovan looked to be recovering, and things were going well."

I suddenly was fighting back another uncomfortable urge to be angry with God. My brain kicked up an ugly memory, a sad reminder of my father, a mean alcoholic. The deterioration of his shortened life and all the family devastations he caused were suppressed only by the passing of time, but still remained locked in my memory.

Marsha interrupted me. "Would you like me to stay on the phone? I will if you want."

"Please do." I was nearly back to crying.

Marsha had good news to share. "In my heart of hearts, I believe God wants me to begin a new effort, taking my faith and abilities to higher levels. The other day, a clear vision of this flashed through my mind.

"A group of single mothers had gathered in a church auditorium to hear a guest speaker. These moms had something in common; talking about how exhausted they were after coming home from work, but still had more to do. Their young teens and children were playing and running around inside the house.

"Make the kids their dinner and get them started on their homework. Lastly, it's off to bed for the lot of them. And then for mom some joyous moments of peace and quiet."

Marsha was talking with an excited voice. She sounded revved up enough to hit the ground running.

"Guess what? I was the speaker standing in front of those women! They were listening and paying attention to me. I was telling them it was time to bring Christ back to the forefront of their family. Make that a priority in your prayers."

I was hardly able to continue listening as a heavy sleep was weighing down on me. I whispered into the phone, "Marsha, I'm only a moment away from nodding off. I'll call you tomorrow."

16

If I were to list the silent and spoken prayers I had offered up for my friend, in my opinion, there surely would have been a significant amount of saving grace accumulated for Donovan to draw on. But was there?

I struggled to push the grief, anger, and confusion out of my system either in words of lament or shallow prayers. How might I ever know where the soul of Donovan Steele was residing? I wondered if I was even entitled to know.

For many nights, as I lay waiting for sleep, ghostly images floated by me – shaking their gnarly fingers of condemnation in my face. It finally hit me! I'd done all the praying for Donovan - yet I never asked him to repeat the sinner's prayer of repentance. I was guilty.

I know God's truth about life and death: 'Tomorrow is promised to no one.' Specific details about an individual's soul and the length of their physical life are not fodder for quick discussion. And where is there ever to be found adequate time for such discussions?

"Dear Lord, please clear up my thoughts. Am I acting stupid? Do I need to understand all that you do, or allow to happen? Why am I making so much of something I had no control over?"

Another day was before me. I felt no peace. Again I wondered; "Does God want to hear any more of my questions?"

His voice immediately settled the matter in my heart, "Be still and know that I am God."

The doorbell interrupted my thoughts. Standing on the porch was a happy-looking Sid Jackson. For a fast moment, I felt a pinch of jealousy; I wanted a happy look on my face too.

"Come on in!" I was so glad someone interrupted the sadness of the day. "What brings you out here?"

"I had errands to run in town, and it crossed my mind afterwards to stopover. Are you busy?"

"Not too busy to invite you in," I said. "Grab a seat."

I wasn't shy telling Sid what I had been doing. "The past couple of days, I've been asking God all sorts of things. And to tell you the truth, I think He's mostly just listening right now because I'm not hearing back from Him."

Sid's words were gracious. "We know you've been grieving over Donovan's death. And though he and I were never close friends in high school, I do remember some fun times with him.

"The guys want to be the friends we've always been when one of us is hurting. Pick out a place for all of us to meet at, and let me know the details.

"Whatever I can do to help you through your pain now, I am here for you."

I was deeply touched. "I'll check my schedule and get back to you. I treasure your friendship, especially now as a brother in the Lord.

"And by the way, Sid, how have you been doing in the Lord?"

"Eric, it would take a full hour to tell you all that's been going on. I really can't get over how my life has changed. I've even started talking to my family about salvation.

"Since the day you and I prayed in this room, God has been telling me something about you. I know that sounds weird. I believe you're going to be a busy man from here on out. His words not mine."

My ears perked up. That was pretty much word-for-word what Marsha had first shared with me after I became a Christian. Since then, a persistent voice has been whispering into my heart.

"Follow me. Obey me. Serve me." I did my best to seriously do that, but struggled. It seemed impossible that a voice so soothing could also be so commanding. It was gentle and wise at the same time. I was sure it was the Master's voice.

"Sid, I truly have been getting busier. Sharing what God has placed in your heart is a blessing to me. I'm convinced it is true. Thank you for speaking from your heart."

I stood at the ready to shake off the anchor of depression. Finally, I felt inspiration again!

"Talk about miracles! In such a very short space of time, both of our lives have been radically changed. And it was only a few months ago you said that you'd be the keeper of hell's flame. That was the night I asked everyone at your house where they would spend eternity."

A guilty look showed up on Sid's reddened face.

"You always made fun of TV preachers whenever you had the chance," I said, in a light-hearted tone. "And at the time, it seemed funny because neither of us had the slightest bit of faith in God.

"But, man-oh-man, look at us now. Two old friends, standing together as Christians! Can the rest of our gang be far behind?"

The phrase, 'Talk your thoughts,' was one I liked, and Sid was as good as anyone to do that with.

I let my pent up words jump out. "Oil and water do not mix, nor will a secular society and Christian doctrine."

For me, it was troubling to watch the media parade and promote foolish people as intelligent and open-minded. "Ignore God's truth and follow what we say," they yell, pushing their zany and ungodly philosophies more and more.

I never quite noticed how bad things were for followers of Jesus Christ until I became one myself. For me, it's a no-brainer. God's Word can't co-exist with any other doctrine.

When God opened my eyes to see the battles waged by the devil, I wondered why He allows such rancid behavior, vulgarity, and demonic attitudes to continue.

Sid was listening to me with his Christian ears. As I looked at him sitting on the couch, it was hard to think of him as a brother in the Lord. But he was!

He set his glass of tea down on the table, and let loose with strong words. "Here we are, a couple of new-born Christians thinking we know it all. Eric, you're right! The world is going to hell in a hand basket. It looks darn near unstoppable too. I'm so glad I know the Truth. Both of us do. But what can we do about the rest of the world? How do we tell the world what we know?"

Twenty-first century soldiers for God? Not these two

palookas. At best, a pair of middle-aged men thinking more highly of themselves than they ought to.

"A spoiled rich kid and a hard-nosed businessman don't make for a very pretty picture," Sid spouted, his stern-looking face beginning to grin. "I'll tell you another thing, all these folks flapping their gums and talking like they got the low-down on how to live without God in their life; well, won't they be surprised on Judgment Day when they find out how wrong they were."

I was impressed at Sid's words. And had Marsha been in the room with us, she would have been too. His comments were solid because he had been reading and learning the Bible.

Not stopping, he pointed out how God uses the least qualified to get something of significance done: "Young David took down Goliath. Noah built the ark. Jonah spent three days in the belly of a whale before obeying God's call to go to Nineveh. Moses was a stutterer, yet led the Israelites out of Egypt!"

Sid's charging voice was rising to the occasion. "In using the least of us to accomplish His purposes, God gets all the glory!"

"Amen!" I shouted, realizing how unqualified I am to be used of God for anything at all.

Sid spoke up again. "I've got something to ask you. As a Christian, Eric, do you have an end goal for your life?" His question was a valid one.

My response was quick. "I'm a winner," I declared. "I'm a doer. I don't quit, nor do I ever plan to! When God lifted me out of the rut I was in and set my feet on solid ground, it proved one thing to me; in His eyes, I was worth saving.

And that means I must believe what God believes about me. I tell the story; He gets the glory!

"My goal is to do all He has for me to do. Honestly, right now, I don't even know what that is." I spoke as if I were holding a revival meeting in my living room.

"Something is heating up inside of me, and it's a good thing. Instead of slowing down and giving up, I'm on fire for God, and ready to spread my wings.

"I want to be Blood-washed, not world washed!" I exclaimed. "This world is the filth I need washed off of me! Jesus' shed blood is the cleansing agent."

"Hallelujah!" Sid shouted. Standing right in front of him was a man being taken over by the Creator of the Universe, God Almighty!

17

The deal was sealed. I was confidently sure that Heaven was going to be my eternal home. I'd willingly done what the Bible said; invite Jesus Christ into my heart, ask Him to forgive my sins, and let Him rule and reign in my life. It's simple enough to say such words, yet not so easy to live them out.

NO! Heaven is not for sale. Scripture says that the cost of eternal salvation is beyond any of us affording it, deserving or earning it. It is a free gift from God to anyone, anywhere who calls upon the name of the Lord.

Does eternal glory last forever? Let's hope it isn't tied to anything earthly, especially a ticking clock. I wonder if our human methods of marking time are similar to God's. Contemplating eternity nearly shuts my brain down with fits of confusion. I can only shake my head at it. I cannot fathom anything beyond seconds, minutes, and hours. Living in heaven with Jesus requires no clocks and calendars.

Marsha once had reminded me that both heaven and hell are eternal destinations. She had a succinct way of phrasing it: "There are no swinging doors at either location. Once you're in, you're in. Of course heaven is so wonderful that no one would want to exit such a glorious place. I seriously doubt anyone up there ever asks what day or time it is.

"Hell, on the other hand, is echoing with screams from souls begging to be freed from their eternal torment."

My deep thoughts were brought to a sudden standstill. Through the living room window, I saw something move.

Hopping across the lawn was a bird. I watched it gracefully flitting around on its skinny, stick-like legs. I was curious to know where it was headed, and how it might get there; having no roadmap, no GPS, no one to ask directions from, and no signposts to guide him.

I remained watching until the bird flew from sight, perhaps to another lawn and then another. Obviously, the bird was looking for food and knew where its favorite meal of worms and grubs were hiding.

It was a moment that made a powerful impact on my soul. It got me to wondering how I must look to God from on high, walking around on my two skinny legs. And where was I headed? My bouncing around used to be for seeking worldly tokens: a classy car, a loaded bank account, and a big fine house.

Heaven is the glittering destination for souls wise enough to have made peace with God. But what about those outside the camp of believers? Just what words are they given as a warning about damnation?

Mark 8:36 settles the matter: "What good is it for someone to gain the whole world, yet forfeit their soul?"

My prayer for more understanding was heartfelt. I whispered to God. "Who among us can fully know your ways? Please place me on your path of learning. I am fumbling around instead of occupying until you come. I seriously want to get going and start doing!"

The Lord gave me an interesting point to ponder: Were my yesterdays merely rehearsals for all of my tomorrows?

I didn't want to behave as an auditioning actor. There is no room for interpretive role-playing. I just had to keep growing in the Lord.

Becoming a Christian isn't a summer project or college laboratory experiment. It cannot not be temporal, only eternal. God was making very sure I understood this.

Yet, I continued wondering how to transition from being my own man to God's obedient servant.

18

The Hourglass Community Theatre, just outside of downtown Milford, was one week away from their Easter presentation. Along with nearly 200 of their other financial supporters, I was invited to a final run-through of the production that had been in rehearsals for three months.

A rich and full-sounding female singing voice brought me to rapt attention. "Oh, such joy! The day is finally here, and it brings such wonderful news. Upon my heart does beat a simple song of joy and glee!"

The melodic voice belonged to the 24-year old actress and lead vocalist in their new Easter musical stage production, "He Lives!"

At the closing curtain, the actors and singers received a rousing ovation from the guests. It was a powerful presentation that would surely receive great reviews.

William Katz, the theatre's owner and manager, greatly respected playwrights, actors, singers, composers, and conductors. Above all else, he loved God.

Years earlier, he and I had become friends. Very often, William rented my trucks to bring in props and other stage equipment from playhouses, no matter how far away. As a business-to-business courtesy, and then as a friend, I provided him the lowest price.

Our relationship was an interesting one. We would sometimes meet for dinner, or on occasion chat with other business owners at charity functions. Yet, it was our spiritual differences that often led us into lengthy and heated discussions.

Until now, I had no desire to entertain the thought that God cared one iota about me. William, however, was a staunch believer. He believed that every sentence in the Bible had a purpose, every chapter a revelation, and from Genesis through Revelation each book espoused an eternal purpose in the lives of everyday people.

I habitually focused on my own achievements, patting myself on the back. William, on the other hand, would frequently raise his arms up and thank God for the many blessings he enjoyed.

How could our two different souls ever walk in unison?

A few days after I accepted Jesus Christ as my Savior, I told William about the changes in my heart.

"I'm truly amazed," I said to him as we stood and watched the remaining guests exiting the final rehearsal performance.

"My eyes see more than they can explain, and my heart is beating like a drum with excitement. I am just a baby in my walk with the Lord, but I'm totally in awe."

William was delighted upon hearing my profession of faith. With a sincere smile, he said back to me: "Have you any idea how fortunate we are? Our planet revolves around the sun, and followers of Jesus Christ revolve around Him.

He is our light and source. Jesus is the one we look to for sustenance."

"Well, you've become quite the philosopher!" I exclaimed. "I appreciate your insights more and more. And this Easter play you're putting on is seriously going to touch hearts and remind them that, yes, He lives!"

William grinned. "You're very kind to say that. Now, my dear friend and new brother in the Lord, allow me to ask you a direct question. Do you firmly believe God is leading you somewhere for a specific purpose?"

"I love your question," I said, "and have been going over that in my mind. I do believe He is taking me somewhere. But at the moment, I'm not sure where.

"God has lifted me out of the miry clay and set me down on solid ground. I see only open roads ahead of me. That is quite a stirring vision. At some point, I'm sure I'll be traveling upon many of those roads."

For the first time ever, we ended our conversation with a hug instead of an argument, a miracle we both rejoiced in.

Later, I spent time thinking about William's question.

"Just where are you taking me, Lord? There must be a destination you have in mind. I want what you want for my life. Is there a specific calling you're placing on my life?"

There was much on my mind when Sid Jackson and I met for lunch later that week. Our conversation covered a lot of ground. After finishing up with some apple pie and coffee, we headed back to my place.

Racing through our minds were valid questions, what was God's calling for our lives, and were we ready?

"Sid, where do you believe God is leading you?"

"I don't know. I ask Him that question every day."

"Well then, we're both in the same boat!" I said. "Do you think that God might have big plans for us? Perhaps He's waiting to put our names up in lights."

My imagination and ego were blowing up. The devil had grabbed hold of my thoughts, but only for a second. Was I going to be a big-shot preacher somewhere or a TV evangelist? I hadn't even been a Sunday-school teacher yet.

Sinking back into my chair with shame, I was embarrassed by my own words. "Talk about arrogance," I said, red-faced. "All I'm praying for is that God takes me by the hand and leads me to the right door."

Sid curtly reminded me that neither of us had yet paid our dues as Christians. "We're babes in Christ, not celebrities.

"God has us where we need to be right now, which is in His class of divine learning. We'll never actually graduate because we'll never learn all there is to learn. I guess you could say we are to remain permanently enrolled."

Sid sounded like he actually knew what he was talking about. I laughed and thought to myself: How dare he and with such insolence?

"Hey, but what do I know about any of this?" he chided. "You've joined up with God and have a few months of introductory instruction under your belt, wrongly thinking you're now ready to change the world. I don't believe that's how it works." His sensible comments had my attention.

There was something I needed to tell him. "Classrooms make me sleepy-eyed. Nothing against higher education, but I'd rather be learning about God on the street-side of life. I haven't got everything figured out, but I am making progress. In regards to classroom learning, well, it's not where I do my best work. I'm better with one-on-one and face-to-face learning."

Sid didn't waste a second. He opened his heart and again spoke forthrightly. "In the few weeks that I've been a Christian, God has immersed me into a deep-lake of realities. I find myself crying at the smallest things and marveling at the hundred things I never paid attention to before. When I think of how great God is and how He loves me, I shudder. That, my friend, is a sermon for sure.

"He has opened my eyes and ears to a new world. The same world I was dragging myself through while thinking I was better than those around me. Fast forward, I'm a Christian now and an honest-to-goodness follower of Jesus Christ. In part, Eric, I have you to thank for that. You led me to Jesus!

"I'm not better than anyone. God is the only reason I have been saved. And that is amazing! It wasn't my works, my wealth, my family name, or my good looks. There is nothing more precious than knowing that He knows my name and calls me friend. I'm saved by His grace."

Sid wasn't showboating. I gave him thumbs up and a proud smile. "You're learning well and reading the Bible," I remarked encouragingly. "Your words have blessed me. I suppose you share your faith with others. Are you?"

Sid answered with a humble voice. "Not as much as I should be. But yes, a couple of times. From the moment I asked Jesus Christ into my heart, nothing in my life has stayed the same.

"The other day, I had lunch with our teacher friend, Gary Owens. We talked about Jesus while eating spicy hot chicken wings at The Chicken Coop. Everything on their menu is fantastic.

"Anyway, he was quite surprised by my faith in Jesus. Gary believes good works and charitable giving will get him into Heaven. I shared what the Bible teaches, that we each must repent of our sins and invite Jesus Christ into our hearts. At least he listened to me."

Sid and I ended the afternoon spending a couple of minutes together in prayer. We were new brothers in Christ, and also becoming better friends. That was a blessing I couldn't have imagined, not even a month earlier.

19

A barrage of powerful thunderclaps shook me awake. It was 5 a.m., an hour earlier than my usual 'get-out-of-bed' time. I loved the solitude of early-morning hours. Reading the Bible and praying were now first on my list of daily priorities. An uninterrupted hour with God was precious time.

The rainy morning became a special one, as God led me into a time of reflection. Not only was I thinking about the most current moments with Him, but also looking back. He brought me through heartache, sickness, despair, and delivered me from vices and habits. Needless to say, my heart was rejoicing.

And how could I ever overlook thanking Him for Marsha? Her sincere kindness and tenderness made me a better man. She always let me be myself. To say I loved her so soon after meeting her, well, that might be a slight exaggeration.

But deep in my heart now, I knew I was in love with her. I fought it, denied it, and hid from it. I was running out of breath on the matter, and growing afraid of what

God might be trying to tell me. I had been covering up my spiritual ears, so to speak. If God said stop pursuing her, I wasn't sure what my reaction might be.

Marsha did retire from teaching. And as she had earlier shared with me, God led her to begin a ministry encouraging single mothers in the Lord. It was well-received and grew throughout the area.

Not forgetting her promise to have lunch with me, Marsha called to set a day for us to meet. We talked with ease and laughed together through lunch. In the back of my mind was the near-impossible decision I was going to have to deal with.

I noticed something wonderful about Marsha that afternoon. Whenever she smiled, her eyes were hard-fixed directly on me. It was tough to ignore that. A bit later, as we stood alongside our cars, slowly saying goodbye for the day, a wave of adrenaline surged through me. Quite suddenly, I made a move.

Without realizing what I was doing, I took hold of Marsha's right hand and asked if she would marry me. As soon as the words left my mouth, I expected her to laugh and shut me down cold. Like a guilty man at the scene of a crime, I wanted to run fast away. I couldn't, my legs went weak.

Marsha must have been in shock. Her eyes were glazed. It seemed a terribly long-moment before she responded. Her right hand was still in mine.

I wanted to take back my proposal, offering her a quick chance to flee away and still drive home a single woman. Whatever was going to happen next was up to her. Nothing I could do at that point would make any difference.

She began smiling and crying at the same time. I held my breath as she reached out to take hold of my other hand, and breathlessly exclaim, "Yes!"

I was stunned, perhaps as much as she had been when I asked her to marry me. And then, without my even asking her, Marsha repeated herself.

"Yes!" Her eyes were dancing and happy. There was no hesitation, no cautious tone in her voice, nor any change in posture as she stood straight and tall in front of me. In one beautiful moment, Marsha agreed to become my wife.

We stood there hugging, almost dancing and almost cheering. My hold on her was tight. She wasn't letting go either. It was a precious happening for both of us.

Marsha's outpouring of joy was more than I could have imagined. Her blue eyes were flooded with tears. Pulling a tissue from her jacket pocket, she dabbed them dry.

"Well, what do you think?" She asked, nearly out of control. I was speechless. We hugged again. I was more than just happy. I was elated! This time we both knew what had just happened. It was a miracle. Even without having a list of reasons why, I loved her.

Marsha took a moment to lean back in my arms. "For years, I've been praying for a husband," she said. "You are the answer to my prayer. God brought us together for a purpose. What a miracle this is for both of us!"

I don't know how many minutes passed before we caught our breath and knelt down next to each other in the parking lot. At that moment, her exuberant words were all I remember.

"Thank you, Father! Thank you! Knit our hearts together and lay your hand upon our lives from this moment forward. May we serve and honor you as man and wife. Thank you, Lord Jesus! Amen!"

Another year would pass before this beautiful woman and I would stand together at an altar and pledge our love and our lives to each other, and to Almighty God!

20

The autopsy report was complete. Donovan Steele had died of liver damage. I had his body shipped back to Virginia. His children and remaining acquaintances were able to pay their respects.

A batch of unexpected business details needed my quick attention. Additional legal papers required follow-up clarifications, and a few new tax forms had to be filed. My signature was needed on each of them. Within a few weeks, all of those matters were taken care of. Thankfully my former business was continuing to grow.

I heard from Sid, who had something interesting to share. He experienced a vision of himself strumming his guitar and singing on a street corner. That was enough for him to ask God some timely questions.

I had a question too. "Lord, what do you have for me to do?" He kept showing me the sidewalk, the street, and the corner from my dream.

"Hit the streets!" I'd come to recognize His voice and presence. It was more than a suggestion; it was a command! That was all I needed to hear. It was all I could think about.

I was the street preacher! But how could that be? God wouldn't use a selfish and imperfect soul, would He?

Were Sid and Marsha to stand alongside side of me as helpers? It was looking that way. They each previously had informed me what God told them; "He would open doors of evangelism for me."

God wanted me ready and available. I actually thought I was, yet discovered something different. Even with a prayer on my lips, my heart was still shying away from Him.

His words were direct, "Follow me, obey me, trust me, and lean not on your own understanding." I'd not yet fully done that. I had only been reacting to circumstances and hoping that was good enough.

Acting on faith, Sid joined me as I visited the local City Hall inquiring about holding a street-corner Christian service. We pinpointed on the city map what intersection we hoped to secure. But that spot and two other prime corners were restricted due to road repairs.

A remaining corner, a bit further away from Main Street, was available with open access. We paid a city fee to reserve the day, date, and location. We were told who the owner was and I called to set up a meeting. For $300, we would have use of a large field adjacent to a long sidewalk, and close to a bustling street corner.

The owner was an older gentleman, and asked to know more about our plans. After giving him the details, he introduced himself with a broad smile: "I'm Harold Emerson. Would it be okay, if early on the day of your presentation, I set a few things out to lend some ambiance to the property?

"Maybe a few bales of hay, a rustic wagon, things like

that. I also have a tall, free-standing street corner post I'd love to display. It was probably twenty years ago when I put my two daughter's names on the cross-plates at the top of it. They loved that.

"During the summer, they'd raise a couple of tents and invite friends here for sleep over's, and I'd set the street post up for them. The kids always got along very well. My daughters and their friends hold many fond memories from this place. I truly enjoyed watching them have such good fun here."

He didn't mention what his daughter's names were. Maybe he'd invite them out to hear my message, and I'd have a chance to meet them.

"I'll appreciate whatever you do to spruce the property up for us," I said to him. He thanked me and then headed towards an old barn at the far-end of his property.

I needed to rent PA equipment, and find volunteers to help get things ready for the service. Marsha nearly panicked when she realized we hadn't yet made any posters and flyers. Sid followed up on that, creating a catchy-looking graphic with all the particulars; when, where, who, and why. In a little over a week, everything was ready.

Three days prior to the service, I stayed home hiding myself in prayer and preparing my message. "Lord, please give me something simple, yet direct to share with people. Help me not to be afraid to stand and preach a salvation message."

The big day arrived. I drove to the site with my stomach full of butterflies. Sid and I pulled in at the same time. The weather was calm. The volunteers were lifting gear and accessories out of Sid's pickup. The PA system was being tested for the right volume levels. Within an hour we were ready.

Marsha came alongside me to go over a couple last-minute details. Sid strapped on his guitar and began tuning up. As the two of them stepped up on the makeshift platform with an opening song, I felt a rush of emotions.

"Lord, thank you for all of this. It's finally happening. Please anoint this service and mercifully bless those that stop by here today. Amen!"

As I took hold of the microphone to greet the first group of people who had gathered, my eyes caught sight of something that invigorated me. It was the property owner's street-corner post. The cross-boards at the top read, Hope and Joy, written in large letters with white paint on a dark red background.

Mr. Emerson was standing next to the post, and with him were two young women probably in their late twenties. I assumed they were his daughters. I nodded and smiled appreciatively over to them.

There I stood, right at the corner field of Hope and Joy, exactly where God wanted me.

A small amount of buzzing and squeal from the PA interrupted us for a few moments. Sid was quick to make the necessary adjustments on the amplifier, fixing the problem.

As I started in with my opening comments, twelve people were standing in front of us. That was more than I expected. Of all the things these onlookers could have been doing with their time, they were briefly interrupted by something they wouldn't normally see on a street corner. God was blessing them with an opportunity to hear about the most amazing gift heaven could give them.

A few more people came by; stopping to see what was going on. It took a good twenty minutes to go through my prepared notes. "Four months ago, Jesus saved my soul, and He is the reason we're here today. I want to share His free gift of salvation with you.

"Jesus paid the penalty of our sins and willingly laid His life down for all of us. He died on the Cross and was buried in a tomb.

"Three days later, Jesus rose from the dead, as was prophesied by prophets of old. On the 40th day, He ascended into heaven where He sits at the right hand of the Father, making intercession for us, and one day soon will return."

I read from John 3:16, "For God so loved the world that He gave His one and only Son, that whoever believes in Him shall not perish but have eternal life."

A few of the faces I looked into were showing interest. Some set down the packages they had been holding. Adrenaline was speeding up my delivery. Marsha signaled me to slow down.

Before closing, I also read from 1st John 5:11-12, "And this is the testimony: God has given us eternal life, and this life is in His Son. Whoever has the Son has life; whoever does not have the Son of God does not have life."

From our opening introduction to the last amen, 50 people stopped along their way to give us a listen, even if for only a moment.

Six bystanders came up asking for our black-and-white brochure. We then had the privilege of joining hands with an elderly mother wanting prayer for her son's troubled life.

And then, exactly as I saw and heard in my dream, a crying voice caught my attention.

Down on his knees was a man, probably in his 40's. I huddled with him as he confessed a long-list of sins. Who was I to hear what this man was crying about? I listened. He clutched my hand with a desperate grip, and begged me to pray with him.

I waved Sid over. The man told us how his life had become a total wreck after running away from God. "I have nothing left to live for," he sobbed. "I need Jesus to come back into my life."

The three of us held hands and prayed. Between his many tears, a sincere and appreciative smile broke out on his face. He stood and hugged me, then Sid. I made sure to get his name and number.

This moment was no longer just a dream. The man went on his way, totally unaware of the part he played in my life. One day, I would let him know.

Happy tears began warming my face. My life was fixed in a heavenly plan that would open doors of opportunity to share God's love. Hungry souls would be fed. The Finger of God was touching hearts. A miracle of Hope became a reality.

As I turned back towards Marsha, I caught sight of Mr. Emerson heading my way. He was pulling a good-sized cart holding the tall, wooden street pole.

"I want to introduce my daughters to you," he said, grinning proudly and shaking my hand. "This is Joy, and this is Hope. Aren't they pretty?

"When you told me what your plans were the day we first met, I knew God was involved. I've been praying that He would allow me to stand right here with Hope and Joy, taking part in something that He masterfully orchestrated.

"This is the day God answered my prayers. I thank you, Mr. Matthews, for everything you've done this afternoon in telling others about Jesus."

I was more than grateful to meet another person God raised up to be part of my first street assignment.

Our excellent volunteers were nearly finished packing and loading up all the equipment we had brought with us. Before driving off, we all stood together in prayer.

"Thank you, Lord, for doing what only you can do in touching hearts. Bless those that came by, and bless the ones who stayed for prayer."

For Sid, Marsha, and myself, the event was life-changing. It was over dinner that evening we discussed what went right, what could be improved, and what other locations God might lead us to in the future.

I wondered how many passersby at our next meeting might stop and grab hold of what they'd be hearing from me, who in a million years never expected to be telling anyone about hope, joy, and eternity. I knew that if I did my part in sharing Jesus, God would do the rest.

Printed in the United States
by Baker & Taylor Publisher Services